RASCOMB'S RAIDERS

Skye Fargo had heard about Rascomb and his gang, but this was the first time he had seen them in action. They were on horseback, fanned out around an unarmed farmer.

"How many times do I have to tell you the same thing?" Rascomb snarled. "This isn't your land." He snickered. "Maybe we should show you what we mean, huh, boys?"

Some of them cackled, and one, Crane, bent down to grab hold of the farmer's collar.

Fargo only had to take a step, seize Crane's arm, then heave. Crane flew from the saddle like an ungainly bird and smacked into the earth with a dull thud. Fargo took another step and swung the tip of his toe into Crane's chin as the man started to rise.

Venting a snarl, one of the other riders began to lift his shotgun.

Fargo was faster. Pivoting, he had his Colt out and trained on the rider before the man could level his weapon.

Skye's message was short and sweet. "Go on, friend, if you want to die."

THE
TRAILSMAN
146

NEBRASKA
NIGHTMARE

by

Jon Sharpe

A SIGNET BOOK

SIGNET
Published by the Penguin Group
Penguin Books USA Inc., 375 Hudson Street,
New York, New York 10014, U.S.A.
Penguin Books Ltd, 27 Wrights Lane,
London W8 5TZ, England
Penguin Books Australia Ltd, Ringwood,
Victoria, Australia
Penguin Books Canada Ltd, 10 Alcorn Avenue,
Toronto, Ontario, Canada M4V 3B2
Penguin Books (N.Z.) Ltd, 182–190 Wairau Road,
Auckland 10, New Zealand

Penguin Books Ltd, Registered Offices:
Harmondsworth, Middlesex, England

First published by Signet,
an imprint of Dutton Signet,
a division of Penguin Books USA Inc.

First Printing, February, 1994
10 9 8 7 6 5 4 3 2 1

 REGISTERED TRADEMARK—MARCA REGISTRADA

The first chapter in this book previously appeared in *Cheyenne Crossfire*,
the one hundred forty-fifth volume in this series.

Printed in the United States of America

The Trailsman

Beginnings . . . they bend the tree and they mark the man. Skye Fargo was born when he was eighteen. Terror was his midwife, vengeance his first cry. Killing spawned Skye Fargo, ruthless, cold-blooded murder. Out of the acrid smoke of gunpowder still hanging in the air, he rose, cried out a promise never forgotten.

The Trailsman they began to call him all across the West: searcher, scout, hunter, the man who could see where others only looked, his skills for hire but not his soul, the man who lived each day to the fullest, yet trailed each tomorrow. Skye Fargo, the Trailsman, and the seeker who could take the wildness of a land and the wanting of a woman and make them his own.

*1860, Nebraska Territory . . .
where fear and lust exploded
in violent death . . . .*

1

Night was still an hour off when a murky shroud of thick fog enclosed Skye Fargo within its clammy grasp. His powerful, buckskin-clad frame tensed ever so slightly as his keen, lake blue eyes probed the gloom ahead for sign of the narrow game trail he had been following for the better part of the afternoon. To his right gurgled the sluggish Platte River, to his left a wall of undergrowth loomed as a black mass against the gray fog.

Fargo's right hand dropped to his Colt and rested on the butt of the six-shooter, a simple precaution that might mean the difference between life and death if he should suddenly come on something or someone inclined to do him harm. There were plenty of hostiles, bears, and cougars roaming Nebraska Territory, more than enough to give lone travelers cause for concern, and he wasn't about to become one of the countless unfortunates whose sun-bleached bones littered the various routes westward.

Not for nothing did men call him the Trailsman, a handle he had earned the hard way. Bloodthirsty Indians, ruthless outlaws, savage beasts—they had all tried to claim his life at one time or another, yet time and again he had survived where others would have died because he had learned long ago to live by three simple rules: to never take unnecessary chances, to never take anything for granted, and to never, ever let down his guard.

So, senses primed, Fargo rode on, his eyes always in motion, his ears catching the slightest sounds. The last settlement was two hundred miles behind him while Denver lay hundreds of miles distant. He was in the heart of untamed, unclaimed wilderness, and for five days he hadn't set sight on another living soul.

Not a dozen yards to the south lay the Oregon Trail, used each year by thousands, but Fargo had neither seen nor heard any sign of a wagon train for the past fifty miles.

An odd tapping noise suddenly came on the cool breeze, causing Fargo to rein up and cock his head. It was repeated, a strange clinking noise, as of metal striking metal. Puzzled, he tried to pinpoint the direction from which it came, but the fog and the intervening brush served to distort it, to give the illusion the noise came from several directions at once.

Soon the tapping stopped. Fargo lightly touched his spurs to the flanks of his pinto stallion and pressed on through the cottonwoods and willows lining the riverbank, the trees rearing like vague, outlandish monsters in the misty soup. He wondered if some of the Pilgrims had made camp right next to the river and debated whether to join them for the night. While they'd probably pester him with questions about the West, they also might share a few cups of hot coffee and a heaping plate of tasty food, and he could do with some cooking that wasn't his own.

But no glimmer of firelight greeted Fargo. No murmur of voices confirmed his hunch. Whoever was out there was not being obvious about it, which in itself wasn't cause for concern since only a fool advertised his presence in Indian country. Still, Fargo felt uneasy. He tried to convince himself he was acting like a nervous greenhorn and letting the fog get to him, yet he couldn't shake a persistent feeling that danger lurked nearby.

The trees abruptly ended and Fargo found himself on a knob of bare ground mere feet from the water's edge. Dismounting, he let the Ovaro dip its muzzle into the Platte while he scanned the woodland. When several minutes had gone by and nothing unusual occurred, Fargo stepped into the stirrups and resumed his journey.

Undergrowth hemmed Fargo in again, so close that slender branches snagged his leggings now and then. He had to duck under low tree limbs, and twice he skirted dense thickets. Rather than be relieved by the quiet gripping the prairie, he became certain that he was no longer alone.

Presently the Ovaro nickered and swung its head to the left, peering intently into the fog. Fargo did likewise, knowing from long experience to rely on the stallion's sharper hearing and sensitive nostrils. All he saw was the swirling vapor. Whatever was shadowing him was keeping its distance.

Moments later the pinto halted of its own accord and nervously bobbed its head. Fargo urged the horse onward but the stallion balked, prompting him to loosen the Colt in its holster for a quick draw. Then he noticed that the Ovaro was staring down low, as if at something close to the ground a dozen feet away. He squinted and thought he detected an inky shape creeping forward, a four-legged creature by the looks of it.

The Colt leaped clear. Fargo had the hammer cocked and his finger was beginning to tighten on the trigger when the fog thickened, cutting off his view of the thing. Impatiently, he waited for another glimpse so he could be sure of his shot, but when the fog thinned a bit he was annoyed to discover the silent stalker had disappeared.

Fargo was fairly certain he had seen a cougar. Although not as numerous on the plains as they were in the mountains, the big cats had been known to attack men on occasion and often preyed on livestock. Horseflesh, in particular, was one of their favorite meals. Evidently this one was hungry enough to risk tangling with him to get at the Ovaro, which he must prevent at all costs. Besides being fond of the pinto, he was well aware that being stranded afoot in the middle of nowhere was a surefire invitation for trouble.

With nightfall rapidly approaching, the strip of forest was growing darker and darker. It wouldn't be long before the combination of fog and night put Fargo completely at the cougar's mercy. He knew that he had to get out of the trees or find a clearing in which to make a stand.

A faint scratching told Fargo the lion was now to his rear. Shifting in the saddle, he slid the Colt into its holster and shucked his Sharps instead. The heavy-caliber rifle had more stopping power than the pistol; a single shot could drop a bull buffalo or a grown grizzly in its tracks.

Tense seconds elapsed. Fargo prodded the stallion into a brisk walk, unable to go any faster for fear of colliding with a log or some other obstacle. Constantly glancing right and left, he came to a bend in the Platte. Either he bore along the bank to the south or crossed to the other side.

Fargo picked the latter. Most cats shunned water and cougars were no exception. He was counting on the cougar to give up rather than get all wet, so into the river he plunged, the level rising swiftly to just below the soles of his boots. The Platte River flowed in a shallow channel so he need not worry about soaking his few belongings. Angling into the current, he allowed the Ovaro to carefully pick its way.

The crisp snap of a twig brought Fargo around with the rifle at his shoulder. He spied an indistinct form on the bank, at the very spot he had just vacated, and he hastily took a bead. Once more the fog frustrated him, obscuring the hazy outline.

"Damn it," Fargo grumbled, half under his breath. Lowering the Sharps, he picked up the pace, and he was emerging onto a gravel bar when a loud splash alerted him to the fact the cougar was more persistent than he would have liked.

Fargo moved slowly along the shore, seeking sign of it in the river where picking it off would be as easy as shooting clay targets. He had gone fifteen yards when a figure appeared in front of the stallion, popping out of the mist as if sprouted by the very earth. As quick as he was in snapping the rifle up, the cougar was quicker and instantly vanished in the brush.

The situation had not changed a whit. Sooner or later the lion would tire of the cat and mouse hunt and pounce, and Fargo was powerless to do a thing about it. Or was he? Acting on inspiration, Fargo turned the Ovaro back into the river and trotted around the bend, hugging the bank where the water only came to the stallion's ankles. Here there were no obstacles and he could make good time.

A crackling in the woods showed the cougar was trying to parallel the Trailsman's course.

Fargo marveled that the predator was making so much noise. Ordinarily cougars were as silent as ghosts. They had to be in order to bring down game. This one was behaving unlike any other he had ever heard of, which caused him to speculate on whether it was aged or infirm or possibly a confirmed man-eater. Some of the old-timers claimed that once a cougar tasted human flesh, it developed a strong hankering for more.

The stallion had covered nearly fifty yards when Fargo spotted something slanting toward him from out of the cottonwoods. This time he was ready. His Sharps thundered the moment he saw the thing. Too late, he realized the shape was much larger than that of any mountain lion. He heard a frightened whinny—a horse—as it wheeled and galloped away.

Without thinking, Fargo swept out of the river in determined pursuit. He hadn't glimpsed a rider, which made no difference. Since he was responsible, he had to do what he could for the poor animal. Wounded, perhaps in great pain, it was plowing through the undergrowth with no regard for its own welfare, and in so doing was making as much noise as a herd of panicked buffalo. He stayed hard on its heels with ease.

Presently the horse veered to the left, bearing toward the Platte. By the time Fargo reached the bank, the horse was almost to the south side and barely visible. Shoving the Sharps into the boot, he reentered the river. The fog was finally starting to break, but not fast enough to suit him.

Apparently the wounded horse had a destination in mind, for once it attained the south shore it sped due west at a clip that most ordinary mounts would have envied. Fargo wished he could see the ground plainly enough to note whether there were any fresh marks of blood so he could gauge how badly the horse was hurt. He figured it must be an Indian mount, or maybe an animal that had strayed away from a wagon train and become lost. The following moment all thought of the chase was forgotten as the twilight was shattered by the unexpected shout of a female voice.

"Lancelot!"

Fargo hauled on the reins, bringing the Ovaro to a sliding stop.

"Lancelot! Where the dickens are you?"

Homing in on the cry, Fargo wound through the trees. In light of the sequence of events, he was totally perplexed. What was a woman doing there? And who in the hell was Lancelot? He hadn't gone thirty feet when he saw someone approaching.

"Lancelot?"

There was a glimmer of golden hair. Before Fargo could answer, a loud gasp escaped the woman's lips and she spun and fled. "Hold on!" he yelled. "I won't do you harm!"

Whoever she was, she paid no heed. Her lithe body sheared through hovering tendrils of lingering fog as she ran, her long skirt billowing about her shapely legs.

13

"Hold on!" Fargo repeated, going after the woman for her own good. With the cougar still in the vicinity, it wouldn't do to have her stumbling around in the brush. "I just want to talk!" he added, to no avail.

The woman's blond hair served handily as a beacon, enabling Fargo to close the gap rapidly. He was only a few yards to her rear when she suddenly faced around, a small gun blossoming in her right hand.

"Come no closer or I'll shoot!"

They were so close by then that Fargo was almost upon her even as he drew rein. The click of a hammer warned him of his peril a heartbeat before she fired, and in order to avoid being shot he hurled himself to the right, leaving the saddle in a neat dive that carried him into a cluster of high weeds. Rolling to one side, he rose to his knees and elevated his arms to show he had friendly intentions.

"Didn't you hear me, lady?" he demanded. Only she was already gone, flitting to the southwest like a spectral bird.

The Ovaro, meanwhile, had not slowed a hair and was still bearing westward on the trail of the wounded horse.

Fargo rose, then hesitated. Should he go after the stallion or the woman? Scowling, he ran to the southwest, deeper into the woods, bellowing, "Stop, you idiot! There's a lion hereabouts!"

A frightened glance was the woman's sole reaction. Limbs flying, she darted past a willow, tripped over a root, and catapulted head over heels. Her smooth thighs flashed pale in the dusk and then she was lying on her back.

"Are you all right?" Fargo asked as he caught up and leaned down to offer her his hand. She was a beauty, with flashing green eyes and a creamy complexion. Plus a deadly derringer which she lifted and touched to the tip of Fargo's nose.

"Don't twitch a muscle, mister. I won't miss at this range."

"Yes, ma'am," Fargo said dutifully, resisting an impulse to snatch the parlor gun from her grasp and give her a resounding slap for her ungrateful attitude. "I never argue with a lady as fond of slinging lead as you seem to be."

"Back up. Keep your hands where I can see them."

Sighing, Fargo complied. His gaze lingered on her swelling bosom as she stood and absently brushed her bangs aside with a practiced gesture. "Are you always so friendly? Or aren't you partial to men with beards?"

Her spine stiffening, the blonde regarded him coldly. Or tried to, but a hint of a grin touched the corners of her luscious mouth. "You're right handsome, mister, if that's the compliment you're fishing for. But good looks don't count for much when a girl stands to lose her life if she isn't mighty careful."

"I told you that I meant you no harm," Fargo pointed out.

"And I'm supposed to take your word as gospel?" The woman snorted. "I don't even know you."

Fargo introduced himself.

"The name means nothing to me. For all I know, Rascomb sent you to deal with us. Not that we don't have enough problems with Nightmare and all." She hefted her dainty hardware. "Take out that hog-leg of yours and set it down real nice and slow."

Although Fargo was inclined to do no such thing, he reluctantly obeyed. Women and guns, he had found, were a ticklish proposition, particularly when the woman involved was fidgeting nervously and might accidentally squeeze the trigger if he so much as sneezed.

"You did that nicely," the blonde said with a smirk. "I bet one day you'll make someone a fine husband."

"I'm not the marrying kind."

"Too bad," the woman said, rather wistfully. Motioning him backward, she carefully bent her knees to retrieve his six-gun. "I'm Samantha Walker, by the way."

"How far off is the wagon train you're with?"

"What gives you the idea I belong to one?"

"Well, you're sure as hell not traipsing around Indian country all by yourself," Fargo said. "And most folks using the Oregon Trail do so in prairie schooners or some other kind of light wagon. So where's the train?"

"Such a know-it-all! For your information I *live* near here."

"And I'm liable to sprout wings and go flapping into the sky any time now."

Hearty laughter burst from Samantha. "My, my. A doubting Thomas! You sound so sincere, I almost believe you."

"I'm not in the habit of lying," Fargo said.

Samantha studied his features before responding. "You do

15

have the look of an honest man, which is more the pity. I want to believe you, mister. I truly do. Back before all this nasty business started I would have taken your word without batting an eye. But three families have already been driven off and two of the men have been badly beaten. No one dares trust a stranger anymore." Her slender shoulders drooped. "Between Rascomb and Nightmare we haven't known a moment's peace in pretty near a whole year."

"That's twice you've mentioned those names. Who are they?"

"I'll tell you about them while we walk," Samantha said, wagging the Colt toward the Platte. "And once you know the story, maybe then you won't think so poorly of me."

Fargo didn't bother mentioning that she needn't have worried about his opinion of her. He'd been quite impressed by the confident tilt of her chin and the lively spark in her eyes, to say nothing of the promising contours of her lush body hinted at by the way her clothes clung to her figure. Without protest he hiked toward the river, wisely keeping his arms out from his sides where she could plainly see them.

"We were on our way to the Promised Land when my pa got the idea to settle here instead," Samantha began. "Why go all the way to Oregon, he asked us, when everything we wanted was right here for the taking? There's water galore, what with the river and all, and a person couldn't find sweeter grass or richer soil anywhere."

"Your pa is right about that," Fargo commented when she paused. In fact, he had long expected an enterprising immigrant to get just such an idea since the area bordering the Platte River was as suitable for homesteading as anywhere else west of the Mississippi. Except for one minor stumbling block. "But what about the Indians?"

"The tribes that cause so much grief all live north of the Platte," Samantha reminded him. "The Pawnees are the closest, but they know better than to molest people using this stretch of the Oregon Trail since the Army can have troops here in short order to deal with them. There hasn't been an Indian attack in this particular area for over ten years now."

"And the Sioux and Cheyennes are well west of here," Fargo said, "so they leave you alone, too."

"That they do," Samantha confirmed. "A hunting party of Sioux out after buffalo did come on us once. They rode right up to our house. My pa had us feed them and give them a few things and they went away as happy as could be."

"This pa of yours sounds like a smart man," Fargo said. Most settlers would have shot at the Sioux on sight and been wiped out for their stupidity.

"He sure is," Samantha responded proudly. "He was the one who figured out we could buy all the supplies we want from folks taking the Trail. Most of them load up with a lot more stuff than they need for the journey so they don't object to lightening their loads any."

"Which saves you from having to make a lot of trips to the settlements."

"We haven't gone since we got here," Samantha said. "But Ma has been itching to see her sister so we may go next spring." She paused. "If things quiet down by then."

Fargo was about to press her for details when a feral rumbling erupted from a thicket off to the right, which in turn was punctuated by the blast of his Colt as Samantha Walker took several steps nearer the vegetation and wildly squeezed off a pair of shots. In the ensuing silence there was a ringing in Fargo's ears. "Those are my bullets you're wasting," he chided. "Next time wait until you see something to shoot at. All you did was scare the thing off."

"Gunfire doesn't bother him! He's stalking us!"

"Who is?"

"Nightmare! The cougar that ripped Mr. Aarons apart a few months ago. The same one that's been slaughtering a lot of our stock."

"It must be the lion I saw a while back. I tried to warn you about—."

"We've got to reach the house!" Samantha interrupted excitedly, motioning for him to continue. "My pa will want to sic the dogs on Nightmare while he's still close by. This time they won't lose the scent!"

"Why not let me have my six-gun?" Fargo suggested. "If that cat shows its whiskers, I'll put an end to it right here and now."

"Nothing doing. You just keep walking."

Fargo could no longer afford to humor her, not when the cougar might be circling them at that very moment, girding itself to attack. He pretended to do as she wanted, and half turning, he took a single step. Out of the corner of his eye he saw her glance anxiously at the thicket, which was all the distraction he required. In a twinkling he was at her side, his left hand seizing her wrist as his right tore the Colt from her grasp. She recoiled in fear and tried to bring her derringer to bear, but he already had the barrel of the Colt pressed to her nose in imitation of what she had done to him minutes before. "Don't do something you'll regret," he cautioned.

Samantha froze.

"If you promise to behave yourself, you can keep your parlor gun," Fargo said.

The offer surprised her. "You'd trust me not to shoot you the minute you turn your back?"

"If you do," Fargo said, "I'm liable to get riled enough to put you over my knee and give you a good spanking."

"I had no idea you were so wicked at heart," Samantha said, trying to sound annoyed but unable to hide the amusement crinkling the corners of her eyes. "You'd like to do that, wouldn't you?"

"I'm not made of stone." Fargo released her wrist and twirled the Colt into his holster. "And something tells me you'd like it just as much as I would."

"How dare you!" Samantha said, her reproach as fake as the glare she bestowed on him. "I'll have you know I don't throw myself at every handsome ruffian I meet." She opened her mouth to say more when her gaze drifted past him and sheer terror replaced her mock anger. "Look out!" she screamed. "It's Nightmare!"

2

Skye Fargo was a blur as he whirled and filled his hand. The huge cougar was at the edge of the thicket, crouched down, belly to the earth, its gleaming eyes pits of elemental ferocity, its razor claws digging in for the spring. As with all mountain lions, it possessed lightning reflexes and an unpredictable temperament, both of which it demonstrated by abruptly changing its mind and bounding backward rather than forward at the very moment the Colt belched lead and smoke.

Fargo compensated, thumbing back the hammer as the cougar streaked into the night. He would have fired, but the cat veered to the left, rounded a cottonwood, and was gone in the span it took a person to blink once. Thwarted, he cursed and straightened. "Thanks for letting me know," he said. "Another second and that thing would have tore into me."

"You almost had it," Samantha said.

"Maybe I'll lend your pa a hand tracking this Nightmare down," Fargo proposed. "I've had some experience along that line."

"Oh, would you?" Samantha replied in delight, and so forgot herself as to affectionately grip his arm. "The men have tried time and again with no luck. They're farmers, not hunters. Your help would make all the difference."

"I'll see what I can do. First though," Fargo said, staring westward, "I have a horse to catch, and to see about getting you safely home."

They walked side by side through the darkness, along the same game trail Fargo had been following most of the day. He was alert for the possible return of the cougar, constantly surveying their back trail. Whenever he turned toward Samantha he inhaled her delightfully tantalizing scent and felt his blood pulse in his temples. She was extraordinarily attractive and it had been two weeks since last he had enjoyed the close company of a woman.

As they walked, Samantha chatted: "There are five families left now, and if the weather keeps on cooperating as it has been we'll all be well set for the winter by the time the cold sets in. Our crops are growing nicely and we expect to harvest twice as much as we'd hoped." A shadow sheathed her head. "That is, if Rascomb will leave us alone."

"Is he one of the settlers?"

"Mercy, no! He's from back East somewhere, and he wants all of us to clear out so he can claim the land for himself when the government officially opens the territory to homesteading. They will soon, you know."

"There are rumors to that effect," Fargo allowed.

"Once they do, we'll have a jump on all the rest," Samantha said. "We have our land staked out and improved on."

"With so much free land for the taking, why does this Rascomb want yours?"

"He's never made that clear."

"Strange," Fargo said.

"Very. Pa and the other men don't know what to make of Rascomb, either. Ma says he's just plain wicked and I have to agree. He always has five men with him, real brutes who like nothing better than to beat up on others. They're the ones who picked fights with Mr. Jenkins and Mr. Solter and pounded them within an inch of their lives. Pa thinks Jenkins will pack up and leave soon but Solter has more grit. The only way they'll drive him off is in a pine box."

"How about the rest of the settlers?"

"Mr. Baxter and his wife are terribly afraid but so far they're holding out. Mr. Morris, too. He's vowed to fight them with his last breath." Samantha clasped her hands behind her back and frowned. "Then there's Gar."

Fargo tabulated the total on his fingers. "That makes six, counting your family. I thought you said there were five."

"Gar isn't homesteading like the rest of us. He just showed up one day, built himself a dugout along the river, and took to trapping and hunting to put food on his table."

A flinty quality in her tone prompted Fargo to say, "I gather you don't like him much?"

"Not at all." Samantha shivered as if cold. "He has a way of looking at a woman that makes me want to run and hide. And he's too free with his hands for my liking."

"Your folks let him come around to bother you?"

"It's not like that. I've never let on how I feel. They'd think I was being silly," Samantha said. "You see, once a week all the families get together for a social. Gar always brings meat or wild onions or whatever for the table and dances with some of the ladies. He's always prim and proper with the married women, but when he gets Allyson and me alone he pushes to the limit."

"Allyson?"

"Morris. She's about my age."

"If she's half as good-looking, I can't say as I blame this Gar for his interest," Fargo said with a smile.

"Mr. Fargo, please," Samantha said coyly, her flattered expression belying her words.

"Call me Skye."

A patch of bare earth appeared, and revealed in the pale glow of the rising moon were freshly turned clods of earth. Fargo squatted to examine the hoofprints. "Two horses, mine and that other one I saw, I reckon."

"It must have been Lancelot, my sorrel," Samantha exclaimed happily. "I was out for my evening ride when he threw me and ran off. He's never done that before. I figure he probably picked up Nightmare's scent and panicked."

Fargo held his tongue as he rose. From her attitude he could tell that she was quite attached to the animal, and he wasn't about to confess to accidentally shooting it so soon after making her acquaintance, not if he wanted to stay in her good graces. "You named your horse Lancelot?"

"From a book I read about life in old England," Samantha answered dreamily. "Those were the days. Knights in shining armor coming to the rescue of fair maidens. Princes and princesses and the affairs of the royal court. How I would have loved to live back then. Wouldn't you?"

"And go clanking around the countryside like a pot-bellied stove with legs? No thanks."

"Men!" Samantha declared. "There isn't one of you in ten who has a genuine shred of romance in his soul." She swayed as she walked, her head tilted to the sparkling stars. "One day my own prince will show up. My own Lancelot who will take me away from all this. We'll have a fine home of our own and a yard filled with playing children, and at night—" She stopped, then coughed.

"I hope you find him."

"Thank you," Samantha said softly.

Suddenly a large form materialized directly in their path, an enormous, hairy man whose broad shoulders were covered by a buffalo robe. Samantha started, clapping a hand to her mouth in fright. Fargo was equally startled, but he had the presence of mind to take a step back and reach for his Colt. He checked his draw when he saw that the man's hands were empty and the giant made no threatening moves.

"Gar," Samantha blurted.

"Miss Sam."

"You scared me half to death! What are you doing here?"

"Gar heard shots," the giant rumbled, his black eyes fixed on the Trailsman.

"Nightmare is abroad," Samantha said. "You had better be careful."

"Gar ain't afraid of stupid mountain lion," the giant said. "If Nightmare try to hurt Gar, Gar do this." He mimicked the motion of ramming the big cat over his knee and breaking it in two. "Gar is the strongest there is." Bushing eyebrows knit together suspiciously, he jabbed a thick thumb and demanded, "Who's this? Gar never see him around before."

Samantha introduced Fargo. "He's a friend," she explained simply.

"You staying long, mister?" Gar asked.

Fargo hesitated. He was about to say that he planned to ride on just as soon as he found his pinto, but he had second thoughts. Even though the problems the homesteaders had were rightfully none of his concern, he was inclined to see what he could do to help them out. Then, too, he resented the hard glare Gar gave him and the giant's arrogant attitude. So he replied, "As long as I need to."

"Strangers ain't welcome around here."

"Gar!" Samantha snapped. "You be civil. Since when have we ever refused hospitality to those passing through? Mr. Fargo is as welcome to stay as anyone else would be."

The giant was unable to hide his resentment. His thumb jabbed at Fargo again and he said, "Suit yourself, Miss Sam. But don't blame Gar later."

"What do you mean?"

A sly smile creased Gar's bestial face. "Puny man not strong like Gar. If Nightmare catch him, who can say?" Chuckling to himself, he headed off into the woods.

"Pay him no mind," Samantha whispered. "He's touched in the head, is all."

Was he indeed? Fargo wondered. Unless he missed his guess, there was more to the strange giant than met the eye. He watched as the hulking figure blended into the background, and only when Gar was gone did he realize the giant had not made a single sound while leaving. For one so gargantuan, Gar was extraordinarily light on his feet.

Samantha gave a little shudder. "He does this often, you know."

"Does what?"

"Pops up out of nowhere like he did. Sometimes I suspect he enjoys scaring the living daylights out of us." Samantha gave Fargo's arm a tug. "But enough about that ogre. I want you to meet my folks."

Less than a minute later they emerged from the trees and Fargo saw a cabin in the distance, smoke pouring from its chimney and light framing the single window. The nearby Platte River shimmered in the pale glow of moonlight, while to the south a few low hills were visible.

"Isn't the view marvelous?" Samantha asked with a sigh. "If it wasn't for Rascomb and that darned cougar, this place would be Paradise."

The trail widened, becoming a clear-cut path that meandered toward the house. As Fargo strolled along he felt a curious tingling at the nape of his neck, a sensation he sometimes felt when unseen eyes were upon him. He glanced back at the trees but spotted no one.

"You know he's there, too?" Samantha said. "I'm sure Gar likes to spy on people, but I've never been able to catch him in the act and prove it." She shuddered once more. "I've lost track of the number of times I've felt him staring at me. And Allyson has complained of the same thing."

"Sounds to me as if Gar needs to be taught some manners."

"Don't even think of bracing him, Skye. When he claimed to be the strongest there is, he wasn't bragging. I've seen him bend a sixpenny nail with his fingers. And once, just to show off, he lifted Pa's anvil clear over his head." She shook her head. "It wouldn't be smart to make him mad. As you no doubt noticed, Gar doesn't have all the brains in the world, but he truly does have all the muscles."

The path eventually brought them to a corral flanked by a small stable on one hand and the house on the other. Samantha let go of Fargo and quickened her stride, covering only a few feet when she was brought up short by something that moved to block her path. "Lancelot!" she squealed in delight, throwing her arms around the animal's neck. "I should have known you'd make for home."

Fargo came up to the horse, and without being obvious he looked for the wound that had to be there. Yet no bloodstain was evident.

"Say. Isn't that yours?" Samantha asked, nodding at the end of the corral.

Sure enough, the Ovaro stood by a water trough, the reins dangling. Fargo figured it had followed Samantha's horse in. Relieved, he had no sooner grabbed the reins than the front door swung wide and the light from a lamp streamed out.

"Samantha? Is that you?"

A stocky man clad in homespun clothes strode forward, the lamp high in one calloused hand, a cocked rifle in the other. Behind him came a mouse of a woman bearing a revolver. "We were worried when Lancelot came back with this stallion. I was just getting ready to go after you."

"I'm fine, Pa," Samantha said, meeting her father halfway and embracing him. "Thanks to Mr. Fargo here."

Both parents gave Fargo a frank, inquisitive inspection. The father appeared to like what he saw. "In that case we're in your debt," he said, offering his hand. "The name is Bill Walker and this is my wife, Maggy. Perhaps you'll allow us to repay you by having you in for coffee?"

24

"Or some food if you like," Maggy chimed in. "I have roast left over from supper."

"I'd be obliged," Fargo said, "but I should warn you that I'm hungry enough to eat a bear."

"Don't worry about eating our cupboard bare," Bill said, grinning. "We keep our larder well stocked." He gazed fondly across the prairie. "That's one of the benefits of being a farmer. Our tables might not be set fancy, but no one ever goes away with an empty belly." He pointed at the pinto. "Feel free to put your horse in the corral if you'd like. I'll get hay from the stable."

"I don't want to put you out any on my account."

"Nonsense. Share and share alike, I always say. While you're here, our home is yours."

The friendly reception impressed Fargo. More by accident than design, his many wanderings seldom put him in contact with simple, God-fearing people like the Walkers, the very kind who were the backbone of the country and leaders in the migration westward. The truth was that he often regarded them with displeasure since they were slowly spreading the scourge of civilization, slowly taking over land that had once been home to buffalo and beaver. Fargo disliked seeing the wide open spaces reduced bit by bit, year by year. One day, he feared, there would be farms and towns stretching from the Mississippi to the Pacific, and the life he lived would be gone forever.

Fargo found he had been mistaken about the house. It wasn't a log cabin after all. Blocks of sod had been cut from the soil and stacked like bricks to form the walls while the roof consisted of larger pieces laid across crude beams.

Bill Walker noted Fargo's scrutiny and said, "Sodbusters, some call us. And they don't mean it as a compliment. We don't mind, though. When it rains, we're dry. In the hottest weather, we stay cool." He gave the wall a smack. "As sturdy as can be."

The interior was Spartan, with a few homemade chairs, a table, an old stove, and a butter churn. Strung blankets sufficed to separate the sleeping areas.

"I've been meaning to put in walls," Bill commented, "but I never can seem to find the time."

After leaning the Sharps in a corner, Fargo took a seat and was treated to a meal that would have gagged a glutton. In addition to the roast, Maggy lavished him with a bowl of steaming potatoes, fresh peas, and slabs of buttered bread. A pot of coffee washed everything down.

The family made small talk while Fargo ate. Bill told about the richness of the soil which enabled his crops to grow so nicely with a little irrigation. Maggy lamented being unable to keep up with the latest fashion trends and pestered Fargo for information on the clothes women were wearing. Samantha sat to one side, watching him whenever she thought he wasn't looking and displaying her fine white teeth whenever he glanced in her direction.

Fargo could tell that Bill Walker wanted to ask him a slew of questions, but to the man's credit, he didn't. Walker did study Fargo closely, repeatedly staring at Fargo's Colt, and as Fargo swallowed the last of his coffee, the homesteader cleared his throat.

"Correct me if I'm wrong, but you have the mark of a man who's been around some."

"More than most," Fargo conceded.

"Tangled with your share of Injuns and hardcases, I bet."

"More than my share."

"Do tell," Bill said, sounding pleased at the news. "Sometimes I wish I could say the same."

"Bill," his wife said in reproach.

"Forgive me, but it's true. If I was like Mr. Fargo here, Rascomb and his bullies would think twice before they tried to force me into a fight."

"Your daughter has told me about the trouble you've been having," Fargo said.

"And we'll have more. Knowing Rascomb, he'll stop at nothing to drive every last settler away."

"Why? What's his interest in this land?"

"I honestly don't know," Bill answered, a tinge of exasperation in his tone. "I've asked him time and again. All he'll say is that we have no business being here and if we don't clear out we'll live to regret it."

"Has he been around lately?"

26

"Not for a few weeks. I expect he went back to Omaha. He does that every now and then."

Fargo set down his tin cup and straightened. The anxiety in the room was practically thick enough to be cut with a knife. Desperation lurked in each of their faces, the desperation of people driven to the limit, of people close to cracking from the strain. In the father's face was another element, a sort of silent appeal, as if William Walker was pleading for the help his pride prevented him from asking for outright. "If you'll excuse me," Fargo said, breaking the tension, "I'd like to give my horse a rubdown before I turn in."

The cool air felt refreshing. Fargo inhaled deeply as he closed the door behind him and hurried to the corral. Instead of going to the Ovaro first, he went to Samantha's sorrel and spent several minutes running his fingers over every square inch of the animal's coat. Nowhere did he find the slightest evidence the horse had been shot.

Puzzled, Fargo took a handful of hay and began rubbing the Ovaro down. He couldn't understand how he could have missed the sorrel at such close range, yet apparently he had. Perhaps he needed some target practice.

An abrupt commotion from the vicinity of the stable brought Fargo around in a crouch, the Colt leveled. He heard movement and the clump of hoofs. Curious, he vaulted the rails and padded silently toward the big door, which hung partly open. There were stalls on both sides, some containing animals, other empty. Gliding down the center aisle, he discovered several milk cows and horses. One of the latter, a mare heavy with the foal she would soon deliver, was the source of the commotion; she was nervously prancing back and forth, her head bobbing up and down.

The next moment the other horses commenced fidgeting. Fargo glanced toward the rear door, which was also ajar and through which the wind was blowing, and wondered if they had picked up the scent of a predator, maybe the mountain lion called Nightmare. Cautiously he crept to where he glimpsed the expanse of plain beyond. Buffalo grass waved in the wind. A few cottonwoods rustled and shook. Otherwise, nothing moved.

Keeping his back to the wall, Fargo eased the door inward

with his foot. He hoped to slip from the stable without drawing attention to himself and was sliding his body through the opening when the top rawhide hinge creaked loud enough to rouse the dead. Crouching, Fargo went out on the fly, cutting to the right, into the grass, where he dropped flat.

The breeze continued to ripple across the prairie like a great invisible hand. The only other sound was the yipping of a coyote.

Before going any further, Fargo drew his right knee up to his waist and reached down to make certain his Arkansas toothpick was snug in its ankle sheath. The razor-edged knife was a handy ace in the hole and had saved him from tight situations many times. He touched the hilt, then snaked deeper into the grass.

It occurred to Fargo that he might be making a fool of himself. He might be wrong, there might not be anything out there.

On the heels of the thought came the muted thud of hooves. Rising high enough to see above the grass, Fargo spied a rider bearing rapidly to the south. Despite the distance and the bleak gloom caused by the moon being behind a cloud, Fargo could tell who it was. Only one person he had ever met was that monstrous, a man who actually seemed to dwarf the horse which he straddled.

"You bastard," Fargo said softly to himself as he stood. He made up his mind then and there. No longer was he in any great rush to reach Denver. By rights he shouldn't meddle, but he was determined to do whatever he could to help the Walkers and the other families. And if Rascomb or Gar objected, he'd answer them, if need be, with hot lead.

3

The family was just about to sit down to breakfast the next morning when the thunder of driving hoofbeats announced the arrival of visitors. Bill Walker glanced nervously at the door and said, "I wonder who could be paying us a visit so early?" Moving to the window, he tensed, then announced, "It's Rascomb and his pack of vermin."

From without came a gruff hail. "Walker. I need to talk to you. Step on out here a minute."

Skye Fargo was seated in a chair, cleaning the Sharps. He saw Walker blanch, saw Maggy wring her hands in her apron and Samantha shake her head.

"We have to hear him out," Bill said. Squaring his shoulders, he opened the door, admitting brilliant rays of sunshine. "What do you want?" he demanded.

"I don't want to shout," Rascomb responded. "You might get the wrong idea. Come out here so we can discuss this in a civilized manner."

Fargo put down the rifle as Walker reluctantly edged from the doorway. He stepped to one side of the window and got his first look at the man who was making life miserable for the settlers.

Rascomb had the bulk of a black bear and the features of a weasel. He sported a scraggly beard and mustache that added to his sinister aspect. A black wool coat hid his waist, but a telltale bulge on his right side hinted at a hip gun.

Four of the five other riders were cut from the same coarse cloth. Their clothes were grimy, their faces smudged. All wore pistols and one had a shotgun slanted across his saddle. The fifth man fancied himself, as evidenced by his black broadcloth jacket, wide-brimmed black hat, and ivory-handled Colt.

He was the youngest of the bunch, no more than nineteen or twenty.

All eyes were on Bill Walker as the homesteader strode up to Rascomb's mount. The farmer hid his fear well. Planting both boots wide and his brawny hands on his hips, he glowered up at Rascomb and said, "All right. What's so important that you couldn't wait until a more civil hour to see me?"

A devious light glinted in Rascomb's beady eyes as he leaned on his saddle horn. "It's the same old story, Bill. I've come to convince you it's in your best interests to quit trying to make ends meet as a miserable dirt farmer and to go seek your fortune elsewhere."

"I'm not interested in making a lot of money," Bill said. "All I care about is feeding my family and keeping a roof over our heads."

"Typical. Your kind doesn't have the brains God gave a jackass."

Walker lowered his arms, his hands forming into malletlike fists. "If all you came for was to insult me, you can leave right this minute."

"Hold on, now," Rascomb said in amusement. "Don't get all bothered over nothing."

"I wouldn't say calling a man a jackass is nothing."

"I never did any such thing," Rascomb replied with mock hurt feelings. "But let's get to the point before you storm off." He gazed at the sod house. "For months now I've talked myself silly trying to get you to move out. I've been polite and reasonable the—"

"Reasonable?" Walker exploded. "Thanks to you, three families have left! And Jenkins and Solter were beaten until they couldn't hardly stand."

"They attacked me first," Rascomb said. "A man has a right to defend himself, doesn't he?"

"They say differently. They say you provoked them into a fight, then stood back while your hired killers held them down and pistol-whipped them."

"Hired killers?" Rascomb said. "I resent that. These are my business associates." He winked at the tallest of the bunch, a man whose crooked nose and mangled ear testified to his fondness for brawling. "Isn't that right, Crane."

"Whatever you say, boss," Crane said, eliciting a laugh from all the hardcases except the young man with the expensive Colt.

Rascomb addressed Walker. "I think you owe them an apology, mister. And be quick about it."

"Not likely," Walker said.

"I'm serious," Rascomb insisted, kneeing his horse so the animal took a short step and bumped into the homesteader. "You took me to task at the slightest hint of an insult, then you go and do the same thing yourself."

Walker held his ground, gesturing angrily. "I'm damn tired of bandying words with you. I want you off my land, and I want you off it *now*."

So angry was the farmer that he failed to notice the other riders casually fanning out to either side, but Fargo observed their strategy and guessed their intent before they had their intended victim completely hemmed in. He strode to the doorway, squeezed past Samantha and her mother, and came up behind the horse bearing Crane so quickly that none of the gang were aware of his presence when he made his move moments later.

"How many times do I have to tell you the same thing?" Rascomb was saying. "This isn't your land. Since the government hasn't opened it up to settlers, legally you don't have a leg to stand on." He snickered. "Maybe we should show you what we mean, huh, boys?"

Some of them cackled, and Crane bent down to grab hold of Walker's collar.

Fargo only had to take a step, seize Crane's arm, then heave. The man uttered a squawk of surprise as he flew from the saddle like an ungainly bird and smacked into the earth with a dull thud. Crane's companions, taken unawares, were too stupefied to do more than gawk, giving Fargo the second he needed to take one more step and swing the toe of his boot into Crane's chin as the man started to rise.

Venting a snarl, the man with the shotgun began to lift his deadly weapon.

Fargo was faster. Pivoting, he had his six-shooter out and up and trained on the shotgun wielder before the man could level the gun. "Go on, friend, if you want to die," Fargo said.

31

A shake of the head showed the man wasn't eager to tempt fate.

Fargo swung around, covering their leader whose features were a mask of baffled fury and bewilderment. "You heard Mr. Walker. He wants you off his property, pronto."

"Who are you?" Rascomb demanded.

"My handle is none of your business," Fargo replied. "All that need concern you is how far you can ride in the next sixty seconds."

"What?"

"That's how long I'll hold my temper. If you're still in sight, I just may treat myself to some target practice sooner than I figured on." Fargo wagged the Colt at the unconscious Crane. "So pick up your trash and skedaddle."

Whatever retort Rascomb was about to give, he changed his mind and jerked his head at two of the others. Together they hefted Crane onto his horse, belly down. Then Rascomb hauled his mount around so savagely the animal nickered in pain, and one by one they rode off without another word. The young one was the last to go. Oddly, he paused long enough to grin and touch the brim of his hat. Soon all that could be seen was the dust of their passing.

"Thank you," Bill Walker said. "They would have given me the same treatment they've given my friends if you hadn't stopped them."

"You're not out of the woods yet," Fargo said. He replaced the Colt and regarded the diminishing dust. "They aren't the kind to spook easy. They'll be back, and the next time they'll be looking to get even."

"I know. I don't mind so much for myself, but I fret awful over my loved ones. Men like that are liable to force themselves on a—"

Walker broke off because his wife and daughter came rushing over, Maggy to throw her arms around him, Samantha to throw her arms around Fargo. Surprised, Fargo returned the favor, inhaling the minty fragrance of her hair and delighting in the pressure of her breasts on his chest. When she pulled back and smiled sheepishly, he inquired, "What was that for?"

"Helping Pa the way you did. That took grit." Averting her

32

eyes, Samantha blushed a fine shade of pink and hastened into the house.

Fargo admired the sway of her full hips and the delicious oval her cherry lips formed when she glanced back at him. Her expression promised pleasure if he could somehow break down her maidenly reserve.

Fargo picked up the Sharps and his saddlebags.

"Are you leaving us, Mr. Fargo?" Maggy asked anxiously.

"Just for a little while, ma'am," Fargo said. "I'm curious to find out what's so special about this land of yours."

Walker trailed Fargo out and indicated the landmarks used as his property boundaries. "I've tilled soil south to the edge of the hills, east to the tree line, and west to the dead tree burnt by lightning. The next farm over belongs to Ed Morris. Salt of the earth, that man. If you see him, tell him you're my friend and there won't be a thing he won't do for you."

Fargo was throwing his saddle blanket on the pinto. "What about the others? Where are they located?"

"We're all bunched together. Figured it would be safer than having us spread out over half the countryside. Northwest of Morris, right along the river, is where a trapper named Gar has a dugout. West of them is Solter's spread, then the Jenkins' farm, and the last plot is claimed by Tom Baxter." Walker paused. "I should warn you. We're all on edge because of everything that's been happening. Some might be inclined to shoot first and find out who you are later. So be careful."

"I always am."

Rascomb and company had left tracks a four-year-old Sioux could have followed. Fargo clung to the trail until it bore eastward into thick woods. Here he halted, wary of being ambushed. Rascomb, he reasoned, might be lying low in the undergrowth, just waiting for someone to come along.

So it was on to the hills. Fargo rode along the edge of one tilled section after another, amazed at the time and energy Walker had expended to plant so many crops. Once on the open plain, he galloped to the crest of the foremost hill and surveyed the lay of the landscape.

Like the shaded patterns on a checkerboard, the plowed acreage contrasted sharply with those strips still covered by buffalo grass. Here and there wheat and corn had already sprouted, carpeting the earth. Against the background of the peaceful Platte, the scene was one of absolute serenity.

Fargo could see two other houses besides the one belonging to his hosts. The nearest had to be the Morris home, the other possibly Solter's. He studied a thick cluster of trees about where Gar's dugout should be, and on an impulse he trotted in that direction.

Near the river the brush was thick. Fargo found an opening marked by fresh horse tracks and ventured to take it although the site was ideal for an ambush. He hadn't gone far when another disturbing fact made itself known; the woods were as silent as a tomb. Not a single bird chirped, not one insect buzzed, when ordinarily the thickets and trees should be bustling with wildlife. He put his hand on his Colt and hunched low over the saddle to reduce his silhouette.

The trail wound erratically. In short order Fargo concluded this was intentional on the part of whoever had first made it and used it regularly. Thanks to the sun and the babbling of the Platte whenever he drew close to the river, Fargo was able to accurately judge how far he had penetrated.

The sudden widening of the trail brought a smile. Fargo caught a whiff of smoke and spied a thin ribbon rising from what appeared to be an earthen mound. He also laid eyes on a big bay tied to a willow near the water's edge. The horse had already detected him but was not acting up. Guiding the Ovaro to the river, he let the pinto drink while he glued his attention to the dugout.

From the look of things, Gar had simply taken a shovel to a high bank, scooped out enough dirt to suit his purposes, and bored an air vent for his stove or fire. Piles of dirt still dotted the ground. A stack of wood had been heaped near the door, which consisted of latticework made from slim branches, most with the leaves left on. From ropes strung between two trees hung the hides of creatures Gar had shot or caught in his traps.

Fargo slowly approached. He had gone but a few feet when the door unexpectedly opened and out came the giant, stooping so his immense frame could fit through the opening. In his right hand he clutched the pelt of a newly skinned rabbit, in his left he held the bloody knife that had done the deed. Gar

34

moved toward the ropes, then almost tripped over his own prodigious feet when he spotted Fargo.

Rage contended with astonishment for a bit as Gar's massive jaw worked up and down. The giant recovered and glanced around, evidently further mystified to find the Trailsman alone. Tossing the rabbit skin down, he advanced swiftly but thought better of the idea and stopped again. "Fargo, ain't it?"

"You have a good memory."

"Gar ain't as dumb as most think. Just because Gar is big most expect him to be stupid." The giant stared at the Ovaro. "But what about you? You think it's smart to come here all alone?"

"Why not? I'm just paying a friendly visit."

"You are?" Gar said skeptically. "After what Gar told you last night?"

"About strangers not being welcome?" Fargo hooked his thumbs in his gunbelt, careful that his right hand was poised inches from the Colt, and ambled forward. "I don't blame you, after all I've heard about the tough time Rascomb is giving the settlers. Has he tried to drive you off, too?"

"Me?" Gar laughed at the idea. "All Gar owns is this dugout. Rascomb wants land. Lots and lots of land. So he leaves Gar alone."

"Do you know why he wants the land?" Fargo inquired, moving toward the traps. The dugout door was hanging partially open and from there he could view the inside of the giant's lair.

"How would Gar know?" Gar replied. "Rascomb and Gar ain't pards."

"You think highly of Samantha's family, though, don't you?" Fargo commented. The angle now permitted him to see into the dugout, but all he saw was firelight dancing on an earthen wall.

"How Gar feels about Samantha is none of your business."

"True," Fargo said politely, maintaining the false friendliness that was so puzzling to the trapper. Then he looked up and added, "I just figured you're so fond of them because you go out of your way to watch over them at night."

Gar's knuckles turned white on the knife hilt.

"At least, that's the notion I got last evening when I saw you riding off," Fargo went on. "Was it me that made you leave? Too bad if it was. I would have liked to talk to you about the situation here." He stared intently at the giant, certain he had put Gar on the spot. If Gar denied being at the farm, Fargo could brand him an out-and-out liar. If Gar admitted being there, then it confirmed Samantha's hunch about being spied on.

Deep furrows lined the giant's weathered brow as Gar pondered how to answer. He hesitated, obviously uncertain of the right thing to say. Then a crafty glint abruptly lit his eyes and he said, "You've got it wrong, mister. You must have seen Gar when he was riding by their place on the way back here."

"Oh?" Fargo idly brushed at a twig with his toe. "I could have sworn you were headed south, not northwest."

"It was night. The eyes like to play tricks at night."

Fargo strolled closer to the trapper, all the while pretending to be interested in the pelts suspended from the ropes. His next words were spoken with deceptive calm. "You like to play tricks yourself, Gar. Sneaking up on folks the way you do. And spying on Samantha and Allyson every chance you get. You're just a randy bastard who doesn't give a damn about anyone but himself." He nodded at the hides. "I'm surprised you find the time to do any trapping or hunting."

Several seconds of awful silence ensued. Gar blinked, swallowed, and licked his lips. Suddenly, venting an inarticulate cry, he took a long stride, his knife sweeping high for a fatal stab. He would have struck, too, if not for the hard object that was shoved against his loins. Looking down, he saw Fargo's cocked Colt, and froze.

"I'm only going to say this once," Fargo said flatly. "Stay away from Samantha and her friend. Don't go spying on them. Don't follow them when they go for rides or walks. And don't try to grope them at the socials."

"It's a free country," Gar rasped. "A man can do as he damn well pleases!"

"True," Fargo allowed, slowly stepping backward. "But he

also has to pay the price if he goes too far. Keep on pestering those ladies and you'll have to answer for it. To me."

"You talk big when you have a gun on Gar." The giant hefted his knife and gauged the space between them.

"Don't even think it," Fargo said sternly, and paused. "You don't strike me as being the brightest hombre I've ever met, yet even you can't be that stupid."

Gar rumbled like an irate bear.

"I didn't have to give you this warning," Fargo said. "But I figure you just don't know any better." He resumed moving to the stallion. "If it happens again, if you bother Samantha or Allyson at any time, I'll shoot you on sight. Keep that in mind."

The trapper chuckled. "Gar is scared!"

Prudently regarding the colossus the whole time, Fargo came to the Ovaro, grabbed the saddle horn and swung up. Only when he had started to turn the horse did he ease the Colt into its holster. The unkempt giant made no attempt to interfere. Fargo applied his spurs to the pinto, and as he did he happened to glance down at the bay. Etched in red across the animal's neck was a fresh flesh wound, the sort of crease caused by a bullet, the wound so new it had not scabbed over yet.

Fargo reflected on the implications as he retraced his route through the maze of underbrush to the open prairie. Could it be that he had inadvertently shot at Gar's horse the night before—and not Samantha's? That would explain why her horse didn't have a scratch. Gar, Fargo reasoned, must have been up to his usual tricks and been following her. But if so, what had Gar's bay been doing on the north side of the river by itself when Samantha had been on the south side? And why would Gar have left his bay alone in the woods where the cougar Nightmare might come on it? Certain things just didn't add up.

Fargo shrugged and put his questions aside as he rode into the brilliant sunshine and bore eastward toward the Walker farm. The day was gorgeous, the kind that invigorated a man and made him forget all his cares. Sparrows played merrily in the trees lining the Platte. Robins and waxwings sang. A yellow-headed blackbird swooped close to make sure he was no threat to its nearby nest. Out on the river ducks swam, and once a beaver cut the surface.

Engrossed in admiring the scenery, Fargo let himself relax. A shallow inlet afforded a spot to water the pinto. He was idly noting the antics of a fish that was repeatedly leaping out of the water and splashing down again when he saw the stake. Smooth as metal, as stout as a man's wrist, and over two feet long, it jutted from the bank below an area where beaver often came ashore to gnaw on trees. Sliding down, Fargo picked up a suitable stick and poked along the shore under the stake until he found a length of anchor chain and the set steel trap.

For the sheer hell of it, Fargo jammed his stick onto the trigger pan. The jagged jaws clamped shut, shearing through the thick stick as easily as an ax would have shorn through a twig, doing to the stick what they would have done to the leg of the first unsuspecting beaver that wandered by. Fargo scoured the bank, located a second trap, and gave it the same treatment. "Let's see how he likes it when someone gives him a hard time," he muttered wryly as he climbed back into the saddle.

Fargo's course took him along the tree line. In fifty yards he came to the edge of a tilled section, the dank scent of the overturned earth rich in his nostrils. He reined up, studying the even rows, glad he hadn't chosen the life of a farmer. Not that there was anything wrong with tilling the soil. He just couldn't stand the notion of being tied to one plot of land for years and years on end. ·

Faint movement in the high grass bordering the field on the right made Fargo twist for a better look. The glint of sunlight off metal gave him a split-second in which to throw himself to the left. Simultaneously, a rifle blasted. Fargo heard the buzz of a leaden hornet as he fell. Deliberately, he gave the stallion a kick in the rump that sent it galloping off, out of danger. Then he hit, jarring his shoulder, and rolled partly onto his stomach, drawing the Colt in a smooth motion so that when he stopped moving he held the six-shooter hidden under his thigh, ready for instant use.

Now Fargo waited, confident the assassin would come close to verify the kill. Had it been Gar? Or one of Rascomb's bunch? Scarcely breathing, he listened for footsteps but heard none. He wondered if the rifleman had fled before one of the farmers came to investigate and received an unexpected answer when the cold tip of a rifle barrel was jammed against his temple and a grim voice spoke.

"You won't be beating anyone else within an inch of his life, you low-life bastard!"

4

Skye Fargo had been caught unawares but not unprepared. The last word was hardly uttered when he jerked rearward, bringing the Colt up as he did to knock the rifle barrel away from his head. All the black powder ever manufactured seemed to detonate in his ears, and suddenly he was on his back with his Colt pointed at a lean man dressed in worn homespun clothes. The only thing that stopped Fargo from putting several slugs into his attacker was the realization that the man was a farmer, not one of Rascomb's bullies. "Don't twitch!" he barked.

Startled by the reversal, the man turned to ice, his smoking rifle practically touching the ground.

"You must be Morris," Fargo said.

"I am," the farmer declared. "So go ahead. Get it over with. Kill me."

"Why should I waste ammunition on an idiot like you?" Fargo responded, pushing upright.

"How dare you—!" Morris huffed.

"What else would you call someone who takes a potshot at a stranger crossing his property?" Fargo asked. "You had no call to try to blow my brains out. And you're damned lucky I'm not one of Rascomb's bunch or your wife would be a widow right about now."

Morris showed his amazement. "You're not with Rascomb?"

"Hell no. A man's got to have some pride," Fargo answered, smirking. He snatched the rifle and ejected the cartridge in the chamber. "I'm a friend of Bill Walker's."

"My Lord!" Morris exclaimed, aghast. "I almost killed you!"

"You tried real hard," Fargo conceded, handing the empty

rifle over. "If you were as good with guns as you are at growing crops, we wouldn't be talking."

Profound regret gave the farmer's bony features a hound dog aspect. "I'm sorry, mister. I truly am. When I first set eyes on you, I took it for granted you were one of those who have been making our lives so miserable. I figured you were out hunting for me to beat me up or gun me down."

"And you wanted to get in the first lick," Fargo concluded, shaking his head. "I understand how you feel, Morris, but if you keep this up you might kill an innocent party."

"I'm so sorry," Ed Morris repeated. He looked at his rifle as if it were some sort of monster. "Oh, Lord. What was I thinking of? I'm no killer. Fear made me do it, mister. Plain and simple fear."

"Next time don't be so quick on the trigger," Fargo suggested. Replacing the Colt, he hiked along the trees, seeking sign of his pinto.

"Hold on there!" Morris said. "Let me make it up to you! Come to our house for some coffee and pie."

"Another time, maybe," Fargo said, concerned for the Ovaro. Cougars did most of their hunting after sunset. Most, but not all. And as if the cat wasn't enough to worry about, Rascomb was still in the area.

"Then how about supper tonight? My Ethel sets a fine table. Please! It's the least I can do."

"I'll think about it."

"About dark will be fine. We'll have a plate waiting." Morris waved a hand. "Hey! I don't even know your name!"

The Ovaro's tracks veered into the cottonwoods and so did Fargo. He jogged briskly, counting on the well-trained stallion not to stray much farther than it had the night before. Presently a patch of white and black, bearing in his direction, confirmed his confidence. Rounding a trunk, he saw that someone was leading the pinto by the reins, and he halted in midstride, dumbfounded.

A lithe brunette in a bright green dress was humming to herself as she strolled among the glades and shadows. Her emerald eyes were fixed on the ground, so she had no idea anyone else was observing her until she glanced up and gasped, "Oh! You startled me!"

41

"Didn't mean to," Fargo said, bobbing his chin at the stallion. "I was looking for that churn-head of mine."

"He's yours?" the woman said, giving the pinto a pat. "Nice animal. I found him back along the trail." She offered her hand. "I'm Allyson Morris."

"I met your pa a couple of minutes ago," Fargo disclosed, relishing the warmth of her palm against his. There was no fear in her gaze, no hint of nervousness at all as she gave him the sort of critical examination a savvy horse breeder gave new stock. "My name is—."

"Fargo. I know all about you," Allyson said. "Samantha came over to our place earlier and told Ma and me about having you stay over for a spell." Her smile was the equal of Samantha's in every respect, only a few degrees more brazen. "Now that I've met you, I can see she wasn't bragging. She's mighty lucky. It isn't often we get someone so handsome passing through."

"It must be hard to find an eligible man way out in the middle of the prairie," Fargo said, taking the reins. She made no attempt to stand aside and their shoulders brushed. Her perfume was muskier than Samantha's, even more enticing.

"Eligible, hell," Allyson declared, not batting an eye over her language. "I'm not ready to do serious courting yet." Dimples formed. "It's too much fun seeing what the world has to offer, if you take my meaning."

"I think I do," Fargo said.

Almost as an afterthought, Allyson commented, "Say. I heard a shot a while ago. Was that you?"

"No, your pa. He tried to bushwhack me. He thought I was one of Rascomb's hired guns."

Volcanic wrath lent color to Allyson's expression. "He didn't? Damn him! How many times have I told him that if he lets Rascomb alone, Rascomb will let us alone?"

"After all that's happened, you can't blame him for being a mite cautious."

"The hell I can't," Allyson said. "There's no need for bloodshed. If he'd listen to me, we wouldn't have any problems at all. What if he'd killed you? What if it'd been—" Breaking off, she spun on her heels and stormed away. "I'm going to give him a piece of my mind."

"Nice meeting you," Fargo said.

"Stop by sometime," Allyson tossed back, a forced grin briefly eclipsing her anger. "I'd like to see you again."

"How about tonight? I'm invited for supper."

"I can hardly wait."

Thoroughly confounded, Skye Fargo watched the young woman leave. Allyson was as different from Samantha as night and day, as earthy as Samantha was pure, as rebellious as Samantha was obedient, so different, in fact, that Fargo almost found it hard to believe she was a farmer's daughter. Allyson's bearing, her attitude about life, the very words she used, were more like those of a woman accustomed to rowdy city life than a quiet country existence.

Fargo couldn't get the image of Allyson's full bosom and the tempting outline of her full thighs out of his mind during the long ride to the Walker spread. Her dress had done little to conceal her charms, which in itself had been highly unusual since country women were often more modest about such things than their sisters in the cities.

The house and stable stood quiet when Fargo drew rein in front of the corral and hitched the Ovaro beside the water trough. Shucking the Sharps, he ambled to the stable for some hay and had just picked up the pitchfork when feet scraped at the entrance.

"You showed! I was beginning to think we wouldn't see you again."

"I did take longer than I expected," Fargo said, spearing the tines into the hay. "Ran into some of your friends. Ed Morris and his daughter."

"You've met Allyson already?" Samantha said, sounding disturbed at the news. Hands behind her back, she walked down the aisle. "What did you think of her?"

"She was right friendly," Fargo revealed. "They invited me over for supper, so you can tell your ma she won't need to fix extra food for me tonight."

"Oh."

Hoisting the pitchfork, Fargo went out and dumped the hay in front of the pinto. Samantha was waiting for him just inside the entrance when he returned for more.

"Can I ask you something, Skye?"

"As someone reminded me earlier, it's a free country."

"This is sort of hard for me," Samantha said, coming so close to him they were nearly touching. "I don't have a lot of experience along these lines."

Suspecting her intent, Fargo merely waited.

"I know Allyson does. But I'm not like her. I can't throw myself at every good-looking man who shows up no matter how much I want to." Samantha cleared her throat. "Do you really find me attractive?"

Fargo tossed the pitchfork aside, gently took her into his arms, and planted his lips lightly on hers. He could feel her body trembling, like that of a frightened colt about to bolt, so he made no attempt to sweep her off her feet and carry her to the pile of hay, as he had been inclined to do. Restraining himself, he stroked the small of her back and touched the tip of his tongue to her lips. Her mouth slowly parted, her tongue easing out to tentatively stroke his. When he cupped her buttocks, she pressed flush against him and uttered a fluttering groan.

"My goodness! That was nice," Samantha cooed when they eventually broke for air.

"It can be nicer," Fargo said.

"That's what scares me." Samantha kissed him again, more ardently this time.

The heat from her thighs warmed Fargo's loins. His manhood stirred, rose, and ground against her nether mound, prompting another groan of unbridled passion. Their kiss seemed to linger forever, and when they were done Samantha was breathing as heavily as if she had just sprinted a hundred yards.

"Where are your folks?" Fargo thought to inquire.

"Working out in the fields. Ma likes to help Pa any chance she gets. She doesn't like being cooped up indoors all the time."

"So we won't be disturbed?" Fargo said, pecking her chin, her cheek, her forehead. His tongue traced a silken path to the base of her throat as his right hand worked its way around to her breast. She squirmed and gasped when he gave a sudden squeeze.

"Oh, Skye!"

Fargo cupped her other breast, massaging both through the

fabric of her dress, and her nipples hardened, becoming twin points of stone under his palms. Mouth glued to hers, he ran a hand over her flat stomach to the junction of her thighs and pushed into the soft gap between her legs. Immediately, she stiffened. Fargo pulled his hand back, afraid he was going too fast for her.

Samantha vented a low cry, tore loose, and dashed from the stable, her arms clasped to her heaving bosom. She turned, racing for the house, her swirling hair hiding her face.

Fargo let her go. When she was ready, she'd come back to him. Until then, she wouldn't open up unless forced, and it went against the grain for him to force himself on any woman, let alone an inexperienced farmer's daughter.

Retrieving the pitchfork, Fargo gave more hay to the stallion, then kept busy by stripping off the saddle and giving the pinto a complete rubdown. Twice he caught a glimpse of Samantha's form near the window, but she didn't come back out.

Bill and Maggy Walker showed up as Fargo was finishing the rubdown. They spent some time in small talk, learned Fargo would be eating with the Morris family, and assured him he'd have a place to sleep no matter how late he returned. Maggy went in first, and the moment she was gone Bill stepped near to Fargo and whispered, "I didn't want to worry her, but I saw a couple of Rascomb's men spying on us today."

"They didn't prod you?"

"No. They left us alone for once. I don't know what they were up to."

"Probably trying to put a scare into you," Fargo speculated.

"A few days ago they would have," Bill said, laying a hand on Fargo's shoulder. "I don't mind admitting that with you here, I'm not as afraid as I used to be. After the way you handled those vermin this morning, I actually think we have a chance to keep our farm."

"It's not over by a long shot," Fargo said. "Rascomb doesn't strike me as the kind to give up easily. He'll get meaner the longer you and the others hold out."

"I was thinking of calling a meeting to get the rest of the men together when it occurred to me that we have a social right here in two days. How about if I sit all the men down then and have a talk with them about the best way to deal with Rascomb now that we have you on our side?"

Fargo looked at him. "There's only one way to deal with a man like Rascomb."

Walker frowned. "We're tillers of the soil, not killers. We can't just up and shoot him."

"Then he'll keep hounding you until he gets what he wants," Fargo said. "Tough talk won't do any good at all. He'd just laugh in your faces. And driving him off won't help either because he'll be back just as soon as it suits him. If you want to settle your problem once and for all, you're going to have to do it with the business ends of your rifles."

"I don't think we're up to that."

"Then maybe I'm wasting my time sticking around," Fargo said. When Walker's shoulders slumped, he added, "I know it's not an easy decision to make. But you have to face the truth before Rascomb has this whole territory to himself. Think it over. Have your talk with the other farmers. See how they feel and let me know what you've decided."

"That's reasonable enough," Walker said softly. He took a stride, then turned around. "Listen, Fargo. I can't thank you enough. This isn't your fight yet you're sticking your neck out to help us. I wish we had some way to repay you—."

"There's no need," Fargo said, holding up a hand.

Walker hesitated, nodded, and hurried through the doorway, almost bumping into his wife, who was bringing out a tall glass of water.

Shortly thereafter Fargo rode from the yard. The Ovaro was refreshed and raring to go. To the west a bank of roiling clouds blanketed the horizon, promising rain before the day was done. The breeze brought with it the tangy scent of moisture in the air.

Darkness tinged the landscape when Fargo spied the lights from the Morris house. Even though Morris was expecting him, to be on the safe side he hailed the house from fifty yards out and received an answering shout. Ed Morris, a tall, slender woman with striking red hair who had to be Morris's wife, and Allyson were waiting by the front door when he drew rein at a sturdy hitching post. "Howdy," Fargo greeted them. "Is your invitation still good?"

"It sure is," Morris replied, pumping Fargo's hand. "Laurel," he addressed the redhead, "this is the poor man I nearly shot today."

"It would be just like you to shoot the one man who might be able to help us," Laurel said scornfully. She came forward, her tone changing from bitter to buttery in the span of a single pace. "I'm so delighted to make your acquaintance, Mr. Fargo. Samantha told us a little about you, but there's so much more we'd like to know."

"Pleased to meet you, ma'am," Fargo responded, taking her offered hand. He was more than mildly surprised when, as she withdrew her fingers, she deliberately but delicately scraped his palm with one of her long, tapered fingernails. The next thing he knew, Laurel had taken him by one arm, Allyson by the other, and he was escorted inside and seated at the head of their table.

Ed Morris showed no signs of minding how friendly his wife and daughter were being. Taking a chair across from Fargo, he went on at length about how happy he was to have Fargo siding with the farmers, and he detailed the problems Rascomb had been causing.

Fargo learned little new. Morris had no idea why Rascomb wanted all the land. Twice Rascomb had paid him a visit, but each time Morris went out to talk with a rifle in hand and Rascomb had not become belligerent. If anything, from the sound of things Rascomb had been unduly polite, particularly on the second visit. There had been no attempt made to assault Morris, as had been done with Jenkins and Solter and would have been done to Bill Walker if not for Fargo's intervention.

During the talk, the women stayed quiet. Fargo downed two bowls of venison stew and added a half-dozen piping hot biscuits smothered in butter for good measure. Laurel and Allyson went out of their way to attend to his every need, passing the salt if he so much as looked at the shaker or filling his coffee cup when it was less than a third empty. Both of them "accidentally" brushed their hands against his several times. They were as blatant as they could be without risk of being caught by Morris, their invitations as obvious as the smoldering fires in the hooded gazes they cast in Fargo's direction.

Fargo gave no indication that he even noticed, although inwardly he thought about nothing else. It had been a while since he'd enjoyed the intimate company of a woman and he was eager to do so again, but he wasn't about to invite trouble by making a play for either of the Morris women with the man of the house sitting right there across from him. So he pretended not to be affected and devoted his attention to Ed Morris.

Later, while the women cleared the table, Morris took Fargo out to show off his stable, which was bigger than Walker's but no more solidly built. Morris also explained about the irrigation ditches he was in the process of digging to divert precious water from the Platte to his crops. One day, Morris predicted, he'd be one of the richest farmers in the whole territory.

At that point Fargo mentioned the meeting Bill Walker was going to hold at the next social, and the reason for it.

"I'm with you," Morris said when Fargo was done. "I'm tired of always having to look over my shoulder when I'm out in the fields. I'm tired of having to fret over my women, never knowing if Rascomb might pay them a visit while I'm gone. If you say the only way to end this once and for all is to put a bullet into Rascomb, then let's do it."

Fargo was glad to have the farmer agree and said as much.

"Actually, shooting might be too good for the bastard," Morris declared. "Maybe we should make an example of him and his boys by stringing them up along the Oregon Trail, or maybe we should have Gar skin their hides and tack the skins up on some boards." Morris laughed. "Wouldn't that be a sight?"

"It sure would," Fargo agreed, bothered by the man's bloodthirsty glee. Morris, as Samantha had claimed, had more than enough gumption to stand up to Rascomb, but he had no regard at all as to how he went about doing it. In a sense, the farmer was more savage than Rascomb himself.

They talked awhile longer, then Fargo casually said, "Well, I reckon I'd best be getting back. It's been a long day and I can use some sleep."

"Thank you again for coming," Morris said. "And from now on don't be a stranger. You're welcome to stop by anytime, anytime at all."

Only Laurel came to the doorway to wave good-bye. Fargo tipped his hat to her, applied his spurs, and trotted into the surrounding night. The chirping of crickets formed a noisy chorus, while over by the river an owl was voicing the perennial question of its kind. He rode between tilled sections, the wind fanning his hair from behind. Overhead, clouds were moving in, a harbinger of the impending rain.

Soon enough the lights of the house faded. Fargo had to bear to the right to skirt rows of corn. Suddenly a slim figure darted out in front of him. In a flash Fargo palmed the Colt and was extending his arm when low giggling and the swirl of long hair revealed the revolver wasn't needed.

"Don't shoot!" Allyson squealed playfully. "It's just us scarecrows!"

"Scarecrow, hell!" Fargo responded. "Pull a stupid stunt like this again and you could wind up dead."

"I was just having some fun," Allyson said, stepping to the side of the pinto and resting her hands on his leg. Her eyes danced with deviltry as she rubbed him from his ankle to his knee. "Don't hold it against me."

"What the hell are you doing out here by yourself?" Fargo demanded.

"Don't tell me a smart man like you can't figure that out?"

"Brazen little hussy, aren't you?"

Allyson gave his leg a slap. "Don't be calling me names! Just because I like men doesn't make me a tart."

"And you do like men," Fargo said.

"Think you have me figured out, do you?" Her laughter flitted on the air. "Mister, you don't know the half of it." She rubbed him again. "Why don't you climb on off this big horse of yours and we can chat a spell?"

"Chat?" Fargo said sarcastically. "You didn't run all this way to flap your gums."

Stepping back, Allyson placed her hands on her hips. "I didn't have to run, smart man. I left before you did and I've been waiting here for over two minutes. Now how about it? I don't have all night. If you like what you see, step on down here and show me."

The wind was picking up as Skye Fargo dismounted.

5

Allyson Morris had the look of the cat that swallowed the canary as she boldly sashayed right up to the Trailsman and molded her vibrant young body to his steely frame. "I knew you wouldn't be able to resist. No man can."

"Thrown yourself at a lot of them, have you?"

"How dare you!" Allyson said brusquely, and without warning she swung an open hand at Fargo's cheek. A vise caught her wrist before she could connect. The next moment her arm was being twisted against her side.

"A man should never be hit for telling the truth."

"Damn you!" Allyson hissed, lifting her other arm.

Without preliminaries, he swooped his free hand to her heaving breast and clamped down as if trying to tear it off.

"Ohhhhhh!" Allyson cried, her spine arching, her lips forming an inviting oval. Her uplifted arm drooped as he squeezed again and her tongue jutted out. "Oh, Lord, yes."

"I knew you wouldn't be able to resist," Fargo mimicked her. Releasing her wrist, he took hold of both her shoulders and kissed her, hard. Her soft lips enfolded his, her tongue darted in frantic fashion into his mouth; she seemed to be trying to suck him down her throat.

Fargo roamed his hands over her straining form, from the smooth base of her throat to the swell of her thighs. Everywhere she was hot to the touch, an inferno about to erupt. When he cupped her buttocks and mashed her against him, she groaned and thrust her hips into him. If ever he'd met a woman who was ready and willing, it was Allyson Morris.

The tug of her hands at Fargo's pants accented the point. He pushed her arms aside, determined to proceed at a leisurely pace. There was no way he would let her get him too excited too fast. He wanted to savor every moment. Her hands went to his hips, and one of his abruptly plunged between her legs to stroke her fiery core.

"Oh, yes," Allyson cooed.

Fargo felt her legs close on his fingers in rhythm to his slow strokes. Even through her dress and lacy underthings he could feel how slick she was. By rotating his wrist, he was able to slide a finger under her underwear and into her slit.

Allyson rocked on her heels.

A few pumping motions was all Fargo needed to drive the lovely vixen into a frenzy. She dug her nails into his biceps and bit his lip as her posterior bucked wildly. It was all Fargo could do to keep his finger inside of her.

For over a minute Allyson was transported by exquisite ecstasy. Like a steam engine out of control, she huffed and puffed and churned until she reached the point of no return and her entire body went into trembling convulsions of sheer joy.

Standing stock-still, Fargo held his finger rigid as she gushed and gushed. At length she sighed and collapsed against him, her warm breath fanning his neck.

"Thank you. That was wonderful."

"We're not done yet," Fargo growled, beginning to unbutton her dress. "In fact, I'm just getting warmed up."

"Oh, my."

In moments Fargo had her huge breasts exposed. His mouth sank to a button of a nipple and he sucked for all he was worth. At the same time he hiked her dress high. She didn't know what was coming when he rammed into her like a bull elk in rut, burying himself to the hilt. She cried out in commingled shock and rapture.

Now Fargo found exercising self-control more difficult. His manhood had a mind of its own and longed to explode, but he held himself in check and began a steady up-and-in movement that drove Allyson over the brink once again. Gripping his broad shoulders, she impaled herself over and over in time to his thrusts. Mutually they built to a staggering climax. She set it off by thrashing like a madwoman. Fargo's inner dam burst, and he slammed into her with all his might as stars pinwheeled before his eyes and his powerful form shook with the intensity of his release.

A few drops of cold rain landed on Fargo's neck as he coasted to an exhausted stop. Allyson, completely spent, too, sagged against him, unable to support her own weight. He clasped her about the waist and raised his head to find the heavens totally covered by clouds. All around them the vegetation was being whipped by the ever-increasing wind.

"Damn," Fargo grumbled, not the least pleased at the prospect of being soaked to the skin. "Snap out of it, woman. We have to get you home."

"What's your hurry?" Allyson mumbled.

"Just listen," Fargo said as to the southwest thunder rumbled. He pulled back to arrange his clothes, then helped her do the same. She was sluggish, satiated by their tryst, and had to be boosted up behind the saddle. "Hold on tight," Fargo cautioned, stepping into the stirrups. "I'll take you as close to your house as I can." He turned the stallion. "I just hope your pa isn't out looking for you."

A steady drizzle was falling when Fargo reined up within a stone's throw of the sod structure. The rain had served to invigorate both of them, and Allyson grinned as she hopped down.

"We should do that again sometime."

"We'll see."

"Any gent in his right mind would leap at the chance to have me."

Anxious to get out of there before Ed Morris showed, Fargo was about to hasten off when she grabbed the bridle.

"Didn't I please you?"

"Now's not the time," Fargo said, bending forward to pull her fingers loose. "Talk to me at the social if you want."

With that he was off. The sky chose that second to unleash a torrent, and the last glimpse he had of Allyson was of her back as she sped toward her home. Facing front, he had to haul on the reins in order to avoid riding over another figure who had popped out of nowhere. He expected it to be a furious Ed, rifle loaded and cocked. Instead, composed as could be in the lashing sheets of rain, there stood Laurel Morris.

"Not so fast, Mr. Fargo."

"How might I help you, ma'am?" Fargo responded, wondering if the mother suspected the reason he wasn't back at the Walker spread.

"There's no need to be so formal," Laurel said, raising her voice to be heard above the broiling elements. She came to his side. "Not when we're on such friendly terms."

"Shouldn't you be inside where it's warm and dry?"

"In a minute." Laurel did as her daughter had done earlier and placed her hands on his damp leg. "Ed won't catch us, if that's what is worrying you. I told him Allyson went for a walk, as she often does, and when he fell asleep I came out for some fresh air myself." She gazed sadly at the homestead. "Ed always goes to bed early. He has to, you see, in order to get up before first light and do the morning chores. By nine every night I'm pretty much on my own with nothing to do and no one to talk to."

"Good thing there's a social coming up so you won't be so bored," Fargo commented, hunching his shoulders to prevent the rain from running down his back.

"I have other ways of breaking the boredom," Laurel said suggestively. "Having guests helps. I do so hope you'll make a point of visiting us again real soon. You heard my husband. He won't object."

"I'll keep the invite in mind," Fargo promised. The frequency of thunder and lightning had increased; the bolts were coming closer by the second.

"He's gone most all day long," Laurel continued. "He makes a habit of riding to the house for a short meal at midday, then he's out tending his crops or digging his ditches until late. Very late."

Lightning struck a tree not a quarter of a mile off and the resultant blast seemed to shake the very ground.

"I should let you go, shouldn't I?" Laurel said, straightening. "I know how dangerous it can be to ride in a gully-washer like this."

"Yes, ma'am," Fargo agreed, bringing the pinto to a gallop. "Be seeing you." Whether she heard his last words hardly mattered. His paramount concern was reaching the Walkers before the full fury of the storm was unleashed. The cause was hopeless, though. He had dallied too long. A mile from the Morrises' he was compelled to slow to a walk, unable to see more

54

than a few feet. And since a lone rider on the open prairie practically invited a bolt to strike him, he bore to the north, into the fringe of woodland bordering the river.

Here the branches overhead shielded Fargo from the worst of the downpour. Rather than press on and risk injury to the pinto, he halted at a cluster of small pines and moved into their midst. After tying the reins to a low limb, Fargo huddled with his back to a slender bole. The risk of being hit by lightning was still great, but not as great as it had been out on the plain. Temporarily as snug as he could make himself, he reviewed the events of the day, especially his stay at the Morrises'.

Laurel and Allyson were a strange pair, Fargo decided. He'd rarely met a mother and daughter so interested in one thing and one thing alone. He was sure that if the storm had not come along when it did, Laurel would have thrown herself at him just as Allyson had done earlier. Maybe the two had planned it that way. He'd have to keep his wits about him when around them or he might make a mistake he'd regret. Ed Morris had already proven he was too quick on the trigger.

Yet another in the unending series of thunderbolts lit up the sky, briefly illuminating the immediate vicinity, and Fargo beheld a sight that set his blood to racing. Crouched at the edge of the pines was an enormous cougar, its piercing eyes fixed squarely on him.

Nightmare.

Fargo drew in the blink of an eye, but by then the lightning had flared out and gloom once again encased the woods. Rising, Fargo glided to the stallion and seized the reins. At any moment the cat might pounce. He had to get out of the stand, out into the open where he could maneuver.

Warily leading the pinto, Fargo edged backward, out the opposite side. Lightning crackled again, bathing the spot where he had seen the cougar in a pale glow, but the mountain lion was gone. He tried to scan the perimeter and was thwarted by the descending darkness.

Grasping the slick saddle horn, Fargo hooked a toe in the stirrup and eased onto the stallion. Leaning over its neck, he rode eastward. At a safe distance from the pines he traded the Colt for the Sharps. Although the storm still raged, he chose the lesser of the two threats and forged on until he judged he was close to the Walker house.

Once on the plain Fargo spotted the dwelling. He also counted three streaks of lightning in nearly as many seconds. Firming his grip on the reins, he hunched low and let the Ovaro have its head. Across the drenched prairie they sped, lashed by the rain and battered by the wind. A burst of light lit the atmosphere and Fargo involuntarily tensed, half anticipating he would be fried to a crisp. Miraculously, he was spared as he pounded into the yard in front of the stable. Fargo swiftly opened the wide door, and once the stallion was safe he pulled it shut and took a few deep breaths to relax.

The saddle and saddle blanket were both hung over a stall. Fargo found an old potato sack and tore off a wide strip to use in rubbing the pinto down. As with every frontiersman worthy of the name, Fargo always tended to his horse first, himself second. He gave no thought to turning in until the stallion was warm and dry and munching greedily on a mound of hay. Then, the Sharps in hand, he made for the door but halted in consternation on seeing Samantha waiting for him.

"I needed to talk to you," she said softly, a heavy blue robe bundled about her white nightgown.

"At this time of night? You should be in bed."

"It's important."

Sighing, Fargo walked over. "What if your folks saw you slip out? What would they think?"

"They're both sound asleep. I made certain."

"But they could wake up at any time," Fargo noted. "And I don't want them getting the wrong notion. They've treated me kindly."

"Please," Samantha said. "I had to apologize."

"For what?"

"My behavior today. I had no call to come on to you like I did and then run out when you did things no man has ever done to me before. I acted foolishly."

"This could have waited until tomorrow," Fargo told her. His soaked buckskins were clinging to him like a clammy second skin and he couldn't wait to get out of them and into his spare set.

"There's more."

"I'm waiting," Fargo said impatiently when she visibly hesitated.

"I wanted to let you know that I won't turn yellow again. I'm a grown woman, not a girl, and it's time I started acting like one. I'm yours . . . if you want me."

"Mine?"

"Take me," Samantha said, and closing her eyes, she yanked her robe open. The sheer nightgown covered none of her feminine charms. Rather it accented the dark tips of her trembling breasts and the dark thatch of hair down below. "Do as you will. Make a woman of me. I won't resist."

"It must be something in the water," Fargo said.

"What?" Samantha cracked an eyelid to peek at him with baited breath.

"Another time, maybe."

Both eyes became the size of walnuts. "But I'm ready," Samantha said in disbelief. "You can't refuse. I've been working up to this all day. I know you want me. So ravish away."

"Ravish?" Fargo repeated, and snickered. "Lady, you've been reading too damn many books." He gave her arm a friendly squeeze. "This is sweet of you. It really is. And if I wasn't so tuckered out I'd be on you like a bear on honey. But I am, and I need to be up at the crack of dawn. So you'll have to wait."

"This can't be happening," Samantha declared, self-consciously pulling her robe tight. "What's the matter with me? Aren't I pretty enough to suit you?"

"You're prettier than most women I've met," Fargo tried to soothe her.

"I know what it is," Samantha said. "Now that you've seen Allyson up close, you don't want me anymore. You'd rather have her. Just like all the others!" Tears began to trickle down her face. "I should have known she'd wrap you around her little finger. She has the knack. Me, I haven't even been with a man yet."

"You've got it all wrong," Fargo tried to explain, but ignoring him she spun and dashed out, the robe flying in her wake. Sometime ago the rain had slackened considerably, the thunder and lightning had ceased. She splashed through several puddles before reaching the house. Thankfully, Fargo saw her

57

pause to compose herself before she went in, quietly closing the door behind her.

Waiting a suitable interval, Fargo followed. A lamp had been left burning low in the window, no doubt for his benefit by Mrs. Walker before she retired, enabling him to reach the corner where his blankets had been spread out without bumping into a piece of furniture and awakening his hosts. Before turning in he stripped off his wet clothes and squirmed into dry pants. Once under the blankets, he was asleep almost instantly.

It seemed mere minutes had elapsed when Fargo heard a tremendous pounding noise. He sat bolt upright, his hand closing on the Colt, his first thought being that Rascomb and company had returned and were trying to break in. Still sluggish from the rude awakening, he saw pale streaks in the sky which signified dawn was not far off, and he listened to an excited voice calling out.

"Bill! Bill! It's Tom Baxter! Let me in!"

The Walkers bustled from their beds, Maggy and Samantha in robes, Bill tugging himself into a pair of overalls. He hurried to the door to admit their visitor, a gray-haired man whose weathered features were a study in misery.

"It's awful! Just awful!" Baxter declared in a rush as he gripped Walker's shoulders. "You have to see it to believe it! The thing is a demon, I tell you! We have to hunt it down and kill it before it ruins us all!"

"Calm down, Tom," Bill urged, guiding Baxter to a chair. "You're not making much sense. What's happened?"

"Nightmare!" Baxter said forlornly. "That damn cat is a butcher!"

"What has he done this time?"

"Slaughtered practically all my stock! Three of my cows and two of my horses, all ripped to shreds by that devil!" Baxter shook a fist. "Right in my own stable, too! Nightmare snuck inside in the middle of the night and tore into them while they were trapped in their stalls! Thank God the rest got so scared they broke out and escaped!"

"Right in your stable?" Bill Walker said, aghast.

"You've got to come see," Baxter pleaded. "I've stopped at every farm on the way here and told all the rest. Most of the men are halfway to my place by now."

"I'll go," Bill said. "Just got to get ready."

Fargo had been an attentive listener. Any vestige of sleep was gone as he stood and announced, "I'd like to tag along, if you don't mind."

Tom Baxter twisted and did a double take. "Who are you, mister? I've never seen you before."

"He's a friend," Bill said, making the introductions.

Within minutes they were dressed, saddled, and on the trail to the Baxter farm. Breakfast was temporarily forgotten. Maggy had thrown some biscuits into a sack, which Bill secured to his saddle.

During the long ride Fargo learned the details of the cougar's attack. Baxter had been in bed about midnight when he'd been roused by horrible whinnies and shrieks. The storm had still been raging, so with rifle in hand he'd dashed out into the battering rain. Halfway to the stable he'd glimpsed a large shape slinking from the doorway and snapped off a shot that might have scored judging by the awkward gait of the mountain lion when it fled into the darkness.

Inside the stable Baxter had found the carnage his nocturnal visitor had wrought, and he frankly confessed to sinking to his knees and blubbering like a little child. He'd invested all the money he'd had into his farm and had none to spare to buy new stock. His greatest fear now was that he might have to pack up his few belongings and leave.

Fargo couldn't help but feel sorry for the man. At the same time, he was bothered by Baxter's account. Nightmare couldn't be in two places at the same time, yet Fargo had seen the cougar at the east end of the valley at about the same time that Baxter swore the mountain lion was at the west end wreaking havoc on Baxter's animals. "Are you sure it happened close to midnight?" he asked as they neared their destination.

"Damn sure," Baxter answered. "I looked at my clock when the uproar woke me. Ten minutes to midnight, it said."

Ed Morris, two other men who turned out to be Solter and Jenkins, and an elderly woman in tears who turned out to be Baxter's wife, were gathered in front of the sod house. Bill Walker once again introduced Fargo and the entire party went to the stable.

Blood lay in pools in the center aisle and streaked the stalls of the slain animals. The stench of it filled the air. All the cows and horses were sprawled where they had fallen.

Wanton butchery, whether by man or beast, was nothing new to Skye Fargo. In his travels he'd seen the grisly handiwork of grizzlies, outlaws, and Apaches. Yet few of the atrocities he'd witnessed equaled the unbridled savagery the cougar had displayed.

The big cat had gone after the throat of each and every animal, sinking its razor claws into their unprotected flesh and ripping and tearing in a ferocious orgy of sheer blood lust. Claw marks were much in evidence, alongside thin strips of tattered skin. Whole sections of each neck resembled gory red ribbons. The horses and cows had struggled mightily, to no avail. Hemmed in by their stalls, unable to break free, they had been at the mercy of the feline butcher.

"Did you check for tracks?" Fargo inquired, scanning the dirt underfoot.

"What the hell for?" Baxter responded testily. He was kneeling beside a dead cow, his hand resting on her brow. "I saw Nightmare with my own eyes. And there was no sense in trying to track him down. The rain erased any prints he left."

Outside, yes, Fargo mentally agreed. But the cougar should have left some sign in the stable. He searched from one end of the aisle to the other and didn't find a single paw print. He did discover a few peculiar smudge marks. Going back to a slain horse, he studied the wounds carefully, making a rough guess of the width between the claw marks and the depth to which the claws had cut. Then, standing, he headed out. "I'll see you later," he told Bill Walker.

"Where are you going?" the farmer asked.

"Where else?" Fargo paused to look back. "After Nightmare."

6

The rain had swollen the Platte. On both banks the water level had risen a full foot and the current was twice as strong. Logs, busted branches, and clumps of grass raced past Fargo as, ignoring the rumblings of his stomach, he rode slowly along the river examining the mud at the water's edge.

To one versed in the ways of the wilderness, reading the signs left in mud was as enlightening as reading a book would be to a cultured easterner. Animals of every sort left tracks; birds, reptiles, mammals, whatever, they all left records of their comings and goings, records a seasoned scout or mountain man recognized at a glance. From a single print could be determined an animal's identity, its approximate size and weight, how long ago it had passed by, and whether it had been walking or running at the time.

In places sheltered from the worst of the rain, Fargo saw sparrow and quail prints. He saw where rabbits, skunks, raccoons, and deer had ventured to the river to drink. At one spot he spied the tracks of a bobcat. But over an hour of diligent hunting failed to turn up a single cougar print.

Disappointed, Fargo reined up and realized he was close to Gar's dugout. A tendril of smoke rising from the top of the bank showed the giant was home. In order to avoid tangling with the cantankerous trapper, Fargo swung to the south, seeking a way through the maze of brush. He had gone only a few dozen yards when a noise at the dugout alerted him to the fact that Gar had emerged.

Halting, Fargo cocked his head as merry whistling was borne to his ears. Gar was in fine spirits, and the trapper's whistling soon gave·way to loud humming. On hearing a splash, Fargo inched forward to a slender opening that gave him a clear view of the dugout. The giant was on his knees by the river, dipping a pair of hides into the water, apparently washing them.

Before too long Gar was through. He hung up the hides, laughed at some private joke, and strolled back inside, slamming the crude door after him.

Puzzled, Fargo continued hunting. He guessed that Gar hadn't found the sprung traps yet or the giant wouldn't be in such a good mood. Shortly thereafter, though, when he came to the site where he'd stumbled on the traps, he was surprised to see both had been reset.

Fargo left them alone this time. He was only interested in finding Nightmare. With the ground so soft from the heavy rain, he might not have a better chance to track the cat for days or even weeks. Sooner or later, he assured himself, he'd find where the cougar had gone. Once he did, he'd backtrack Nightmare to the lion's lair and put an end to its ravages once and for all.

The sun climbed steadily higher. Fargo guessed he was due north of the Walker farm, about back where he had started the day, when a series of impressions caught his eye. Sliding down, he couldn't resist a smile.

As plain as day in the soft earth were the prints of the huge cat, the four toe pads on each foot arranged in a curved row in front of the larger, triangular heel pads. Unlike the tracks of wolves and coyotes, which always showed claws, there were no claw marks since cats kept their claws retracted except when fighting or bringing down game. These prints were ample testimony to Nightmare's size. Where an ordinary mountain lion would leave a track about three inches long and three and a half inches wide, these were four inches in length and over five inches wide. Their depth proved that Nightmare weighed well over three hundred pounds. A monster, if ever there was one.

Fargo hefted the reins and was set to climb on the stallion when additional tracks a few feet farther east made him gape in bewilderment. "What the hell?" he blurted, going up to them and sinking to one knee. These were tiny replicas of the huge prints, three different sets.

Now that Fargo had the trail, he moved more briskly. Nightmare had headed south, skirting the Walker house and bearing toward the distant hills. Although Fargo frequently lost the tracks, he was always able to find them again farther on. And by the middle of the afternoon he was on a game trail that wound among the low hills to one that was covered with dense brush.

Ground-hitching the stallion, Fargo verified he had a cartridge in the Sharps, pulled back the hammer, and set the trigger before climbing cautiously upward. The grassy ground yielded few tracks, which didn't matter because he knew what he was looking for and where he would find it. Two-thirds of the way to the top he found a projecting shelf screened by a thorny thicket.

Fargo took a gamble. Crouching, he eased into the thicket, parting the limbs one at a time, pausing often to simply squat and listen. Faint mewing confirmed his suspicion. Presently a shadowy hole materialized under the shelf. As he lowered onto his elbows and knees, an ominous growl warned him his presence had been detected.

The thicket thinned. Fargo stopped at the edge of the cave opening, unwilling to provoke a charge if he could avoid doing so. Stray sunbeams afforded enough light for him to see the great, tawny figure crouched a dozen feet away, its eyes blazing in bestial fury at the intrusion into its sanctuary. Behind the mountain lion moved three cubs, their tiny tails bobbing as they pranced in carefree abandon. At that age all they cared about was playing, and not even their mother's throaty growls could silence them.

"This makes three times, old girl," Fargo said soothingly, aware from long experience that nervous wild animals were often calmed by such tones. "And even here you won't attack. Makes me think I was wrong about you that first night. You were just curious."

Nightmare uttered a drawn-out snarl.

"Don't do something we'll both regret," Fargo said, backing out. He had accomplished what he had set out to do, but in doing so he had learned there was much more to the situation than he had thought. If the farmers learned he had been this close to Nightmare and hadn't put a slug through the mountain lion's brain, they'd probably tar and feather him. But he wasn't about to kill an innocent creature, human or otherwise.

The ride to the Walkers' was spent in deep thought. Bill was milking a cow when Fargo entered the stable.

"There you are! How did it go? Can we breathe easier tonight?"

"Afraid not," Fargo said, leading the pinto to its stall.

"Damn. That's a shame. We were all hoping." Walker licked a drop of milk from the tip of a finger. "Tom Baxter has had enough," he said glumly. "Between Rascomb and Nightmare he can't take any more, so he's leaving within the week. Going back East where folks are civilized, as he put it."

"And the rest of you?"

"We're staying. But I have to be honest. None of us can stand to lose our stock. Nightmare could ruin every one of us if we don't find that stinking cat and kill him."

"Her," Fargo amended.

"What?"

"Nightmare is a female. With cubs."

"You saw their tracks?" Bill said, standing. When Fargo nodded, he shook his head in disgust. "That's even worse. It means Nightmare has more mouths to feed. I think we should organize a hunt tomorrow and stay out until we put an end to her slaughter."

"No."

"I beg your pardon?"

"Leave Nightmare alone for the time being."

"Do you know what you're asking?"

"Yes."

Bill Walker came to the stall. "I don't think you do. Our entire livelihoods are at stake. Without our milk cows and plow horses we stand to lose everything. *Everything.* The welfare of our families depends on us doing the right thing."

"Which is why I'm asking you to wait a few days before you go after the mountain lion," Fargo said as he unfastened a cinch.

"What difference will a few days make?"

"I need time to do some more checking around. In the meantime, have all the farmers keep their animals locked inside at night.

"We already agreed to take that precaution. Baxter had left the rear door to his stable braced open with a bale of straw for ventilation and somehow that damned cougar squeezed through. None of us want to make the same mistake." Walker studied his guest a few moments. "Why do I have a hunch you know something you're not telling me?"

"I might, but I don't have proof yet." Fargo draped his saddle over the top of the stall.

"Can't you give me a clue?"

"Not yet," Fargo answered. "But when I know more, you'll be the first one I tell."

Satisfied, Walker nodded and resumed milking. Fargo went to the house. The tantalizing aroma of roasting meat met him at the entrance. His mouth watering, he went in and was surprised to see Allyson Morris chatting with Samantha at the table. Over by the pot-bellied stove Maggy was busy chopping carrots into a pot. "Howdy, ladies," he greeted them as he leaned his Sharps in the corner reserved for his gear.

"I'll have supper ready in half an hour," Maggy said. "Can you wait until then?"

"I'll try, ma'am," Fargo answered, going to the counter to pour a glass of water from the pitcher. Both younger women were eyeing him with amused smirks. "Had a busy day, ladies?" he asked.

"We've been baking pies and fixing preserves and such for the social," Samantha said. "Allyson is going to stay the night and help us finish up in the morning."

"These girls have been working right hard," Maggy confirmed. "One day they'll make some young men fine wives." Chuckling, she winked at Fargo.

"Mother," Samantha declared. "Skye has already made it abundantly clear he has no interest whatsoever in tying the knot. He has too much wanderlust in his system to even think of settling down."

"True," Fargo conceded.

Allyson showed her even white teeth. "We don't hold it against you. Some people are the marrying kind, some aren't. Myself, I expect it will be a good many years before I'm ready to tie my apron strings to just one man."

Maggy wagged a wooden spoon. "If your mother could hear

you! She has big plans for you along those lines, young lady. Told me so herself."

"I wouldn't put a lot of stock in what my ma says," Allyson responded. "She and I don't always see eye to eye. And I can tell you now I aim to live my life as I please and not as she wants me to."

"She'd never force you to do anything against your will," Maggy commented.

"If you only knew!" Allyson replied.

"Now hush, girl," Maggy said. "I won't have you speaking ill of her. She's the best friend I have."

Only Fargo had any inkling of why Allyson cackled hysterically, and he suspected there was more to her reaction than even he knew. The women began chatting about the upcoming social, so he excused himself and stepped outdoors. From the corner of the house he enjoyed an unobstructed view of the western sky, painted red, orange, and yellow by the setting sun. When the door opened he didn't bother turning.

"I suppose you're mad at me after how I acted last night," Samantha said quietly at his elbow.

"Shouldn't you be inside with your friend?"

"She's helping Ma." Samantha touched his arm. "And don't evade the question. Are you mad at me or not?"

"I have no call to be."

"Then I still have a chance."

"To what? Be ravished?" Fargo responded, and laughed.

"You think I behave childishly at times, don't you?" Samantha snapped.

Finally Fargo turned. "I think you should do yourself a favor and wait for your knight in shining armor to come along. It's not me."

"I know that now."

"But you still—" Fargo said, and cut off when the door opened again and out waltzed Allyson, her smug expression a trifle galling.

"What have we here? The two of you whispering? If I didn't know better, I'd swear you must be lovers."

Samantha turned beet red. "We are not!" she said defensively. "Must you be so crude all the time?"

"Simmer down," Allyson said. "I was just joshing." Her

hips swung enticingly as she moved close to Fargo. "*He* knows I'm harmless. Don't you, big man?"

"As harmless as a coiled rattler," Fargo stated. Exasperated by the notion of having to abide their antics the rest of the night, he jammed his hands in his pockets and took a stroll into the nearby field, which Walker hadn't tilled so his animals would have feed handy. As if the petty bickering of the women wasn't enough of a bother, events simply weren't proceeding quite fast enough to suit him. He resolved to bring matters to a head the very next day by going out after Rascomb. Then he remembered that the social was the next day and the farmers had expected him to be on hand to discuss how best to settle their problem. In annoyance he kicked at a clump of buffalo grass.

"Skye? Where are you going?"

Fargo glanced around at Samantha, who was beckoning him to come back. At the self-same split-second a rifle boomed in the trees to the north and something nipped at his earlobe. He promptly took a stride and dived into the grass, beating the second shot by a hair. Samantha screamed and someone else shouted his name. Hugging the ground, Fargo snaked toward the trees, freezing when the unseen killer fired twice more. Answering shots came from the house or the stable. Taking advantage of the covering fire, Fargo rose and sprinted in an erratic, weaving pattern. In the woods the gunman cut loose, but he rushed his aim and missed.

Going to ground again, Fargo located the rifleman's position by the telltale gunsmoke. Slanting to the left, he painstakingly worked his way forward until he was close enough to a willow to reach it in several bounds. No gunfire sounded when he burst from cover, and once crouched behind the trunk he scoured the undergrowth for his enemy. A solitary mosquito was the only sign of life.

Fargo circled around, coming up on the spot where the gunsmoke hovered from the rear. Spent cartridges were all he found. He was leaning over a set of footprints when hoofbeats heralded the killer's getaway. Darting to a small clearing, he spotted a lone rider hastening westward. He brought the Colt up, positive he could bring the man down despite the range.

Only it wasn't a man. He saw long red hair flying in the wind and the shock caused him to hold his fire.

Naturally Fargo had thought one of Rascomb's men was responsible. Or perhaps Gar, who might have been spying on the women and been unable to resist a golden opportunity. The last person he would have expected it to be was the one he saw: Laurel Morris.

"Fargo? Are you all right?"

There was a crashing in the brush and Bill Walker appeared, nearly out of breath from having run from the farmhouse.

"I'm fine."

"He didn't wing you? I thought he might have when you disappeared." Bill looked to the right and the left. "Did you nail the bushwhacker?"

"No," Fargo said, holstering the Colt.

"Darn. Too bad. I bet it was Rascomb or one of his bunch."

"That's a good guess," Fargo responded, keeping the secret to himself.

The three women showed and started to talk at the same time. Fargo silenced them with a gesture and declared, "Whoever it was must have been a rotten shot. They're long gone, so let's head back."

"You're making a habit of attracting lead," Allyson remarked impishly. "First my pa, now this. Seems like there are folks who can't wait to plant you."

"I must have a knack," Fargo said, doing his best not to let his resentment show. He wondered if Allyson had known about the ambush? If perhaps Allyson was a party to it somehow? Another thought struck him, one so troubling he broke his stride. What if the incident with Ed Morris hadn't been an accident? What if Morris had known who he was all along and had deliberately tried to gun him down?

Fargo trailed the rest to the house, hardly paying attention to the excited chatter of the women and Walker. He was fed up with being played for a fool. The more he thought about how close Laurel had come to doing him in, the madder he became. So mad, that when they reached the house he stalked inside, grabbed the Sharps, and hurried to the stable to saddle the Ovaro. The Walkers and Allyson were waiting in front when he came out.

"Where are you off to?" Bill asked.

"To get some answers," Fargo said.

"But it will be dark soon and supper is about ready," Maggy commented. "Can't it wait until tomorrow?"

"No," Fargo growled, kneeing the pinto into a gallop. He headed straight for the Morris farm, arriving just as the sun sank from sight. There were lamps glowing in the house, but otherwise all was deathly still. Dismounting far enough away to avoid being heard, Fargo shucked the Sharps and worked his way to the northeast corner of the structure. The clink of pots and pans confirmed someone was home. Tiptoeing to the door, he rapped twice so hard the entire door shook. Then, without waiting to be bidden, he worked the latch and shoved.

Laurel was in the act of setting a pot on the stove. She whirled around, panic-stricken, and gasped. "Fargo. What a pleasant surprise."

"Is it?" Fargo said, checking the interior before entering. "Where's your husband?"

"Ed's not back yet. I expect him any minute." Laurel made a transparent effort to calm herself. "You should have come earlier, handsome. Like I wanted you to."

"You're a bit late getting supper on, aren't you?" Fargo demanded, crossing to the stove.

Laurel shrugged. "I forgot about the time." She grinned feebly and put the pot down. "You know how it is. I was so busy knitting, I lost track."

"Knitting what? A rifle?"

"I don't understand."

Fargo slapped her. He swept his right hand up and caught her flush on the cheek, staggering her into the wall. Stunned, she clasped a hand to her stinging face, fear creeping into her eyes. "Why?" Fargo asked.

"What—?"

Fargo slapped her again, harder this time, causing her knees to buckle. She had to fling an arm against the wall for support. "Why?" he repeated sternly.

"Why what?" Laurel replied, playing the part of a confused innocent. "You march into my house and start hitting me for no—"

Again Fargo slapped her, the hardest blow yet, driving her

to her knees. Laurel gaped up at him, moisture filling her eyes, her cheek as red as scarlet silk.

"Why did you try to shoot me?" he demanded.

"I didn't!" Laurel protested, but when she saw his hand lift for another blow she cringed and exclaimed, "Wait! Don't! I'll tell you whatever you want to know!"

"Make it quick," Fargo said. "I've plumb run out of patience, you lying bitch."

"Let me catch my breath," Laurel said, glancing around the room as if seeking something she could use against him. "My jaw is so sore, I can barely move my mouth."

Venting a snarl that would have done justice to Nightmare, Fargo lunged, seized her by the wrist, and yanked her roughly to her feet. "I wouldn't play any more games, lady, if I was you." Pushing her into the wall, he added, "I want the truth, and I want it now." He twisted her wrist, eliciting a sharp cry. "Why did you bushwhack me?"

"All right!" Laurel wailed. "All right! Stop hurting me."

"Then talk."

The pink tip of Laurel's tongue flicked over her lips. "I did it to keep you away from my daughter."

With a snort of contempt, Fargo whirled and hurled Laurel into the table. She smashed into a chair and barely stayed upright. "I want the truth," Fargo stressed. "Your daughter was throwing herself at men long before I came along. There has to be another reason."

"Why won't you believe me?" Laurel whined, recoiling in terror when he moved toward her. "Allyson thinks she's in love with you and she wants to leave with you when you go."

"Like hell she does," Fargo countered, snatching the redhead's wrist again. "The only person Allyson loves is herself." He gave a squeeze that made Laurel cringe. "This is the last time I'm going to ask politely." Leaning over her, he roared out, "*Why,* damn you?"

Whatever answer Laurel Morris might have made was forestalled by a furious oath from the doorway, and Fargo glanced up just as Ed Morris sprang at him with a rifle upraised to bash in his skull.

7

The stark rage contorting Ed Morris's features was all the proof Fargo needed that trying to reason with the man was out of the question. Not that Fargo had the time. He was forced to let go of Laurel and leap back as Ed swung the rifle in a vicious arc. The stock crashed into the table and shattered the wood. In a swift leap Fargo caught hold of the rifle and tried to wrench it loose, but Morris clung to the gun, attempting to ram the butt end into Fargo's stomach. Fargo released the Sharps so he could grasp the rifle with both hands and for a few seconds they silently struggled for possession of the weapon.

Fargo could hardly blame Morris for being incensed. How else was the farmer supposed to react on arriving home to find his wife apparently being assaulted? He twisted with all his might, felt Ed's fingers slip, and twisted once more. The rifle came free. Simultaneously, Ed Morris pounced, wrapping both brawny hands around Fargo's throat while knocking Fargo rearward into the stove.

Farmers were notoriously strong. Ed Morris, who lacked an exceptional build, still had muscles of steel, particularly in his hands and wrists. This Fargo learned the hard way as he felt Morris's fingers gouging into his throat. He tried prying them off, but they were clamped fast. It was like having his neck trapped in a vise. He inhaled, but no air filled his lungs. In desperation he whipped a knee into Ed's stomach, doubling Morris over, and pushed.

The farmer tottered into the kitchen counter. Aflame with rage, he looked down, saw a meat cleaver lying to one side, and clutched the handle.

"Ed, wait—," Fargo said, and had to duck when Morris delivered a blow that would have decapitated him had it connected. He darted to the left, nearly losing some fingers to another swing.

"You bastard!" Ed screeched, closing in and wielding the cleaver wildly. "How dare you lay a hand on her!"

"Calm down!" Fargo urged. But he might as well have been trying to soothe a grizzly. Morris flailed away, narrowly missing time after time. Fargo retreated the whole while, moving around the table. Lifting a chair, he blocked the next few swipes, the cleaver biting chunks out of the chair with every stroke.

Fargo knew he had to do something quickly. He couldn't evade the cleaver forever. So, when the keen edge of the cleaver sliced into the chair the next time, he suddenly thrust the chair into Ed's chest, driving Morris backward into the table. Ed's knees caught on top and he fell onto his back, his arms outflung, allowing Fargo to throw the chair down and spring.

Ed was lifting the cleaver to strike when Fargo's hands closed on the farmer's wrists. "I'll kill you!" Ed cried, struggling ferociously.

"Damn you!" Fargo thundered as they rolled across the table. "Just hear me out!"

But the farmer was in no mood for words. His teeth exposed as if he was going to bite, he tugged and heaved, striving to break loose.

Fargo saw the edge of the table loom before them. Ed's knee battered his groin, sending acute pain lancing through his body. He lost his hold on Morris's wrist just as they fell. Air fanned his cheeks, and then he smacked onto his side. Certain Ed would be on him in a flash, he surged into a crouch.

Ed Morris was flat on his stomach, one arm underneath his chest, his elbow bent at an odd angle. He glanced up, soundlessly worked his lips, and slowly began to rise.

Mystified, Fargo tensed for their next clash. He saw red drops splatter on the floor, then saw the cleaver jutting from the farmer's chest. "No!" he declared, grabbing Morris by the shoulder. "Why the hell didn't you listen? I didn't want this."

A stupefied look came over Ed. He swallowed, or tried to, and crimson spittle bubbled forth. Gazing in dismay at his chest, he started shaking uncontrollably. "No," he blubbered softly. "Please, no."

Anxious to render aid, Fargo lowered Morris to the floor. "Lie still," he advised. "Your wife and I will do what we can."

"Laurel?" Ed said, his eyes searching the room.

Not until that moment did Fargo realize the woman was gone. In the distance hoofs drummed. "Hell!" he spat. "She ran out on you."

"Laurel?" Ed said again, more weakly than before. He grit his teeth and focused on Fargo. "Why, man? What was this all about?"

"She tried to shoot me."

"My wife?"

"Why, Ed? I need to know why."

"She'd never—" Morris said, getting no further before a coughing fit shook him from head to toe. At length he subsided and lay still, wheezing.

"Give me a reason," Fargo pressed him. "I've never done anything to you people."

Ed was staring vacantly at the ceiling. Blood trickled from under the cleaver, forming a pool on his stomach.

"Can you hear me?" Fargo asked, resisting an impulse to give the man a shake. "What does Laurel have against me?"

"Not you," Ed whispered.

"Yes, me. She tried to ambush me over at Walker's."

"Me," Ed said.

"I'm wasting my time," Fargo muttered, sitting back on his haunches. There was nothing he could do for the doomed man. He felt helpless and not a little vexed by his accidental part in the tragedy.

"Never did take to the farming life," Ed went on breathlessly. "Hated it. Guess I can't blame her." He sucked in a deep breath. "Sorry, Fargo. My temper and all."

"You're not the one who should be sorry," Fargo corrected him. "I reckon I shouldn't have barged on in here the way I did."

"My fault," Ed said. "It's hard to make an angel out of a fallen dove. She was better off as a madam."

"You married a whore?"

"She liked men too much. That was her one fault."

Fargo had a host of questions he wanted to ask. But Ed abruptly clutched at himself, gurgled noisily, and stiffened. "Hold on," Fargo said. "Try to hold on."

The farmer offered no response. Eyes wide, lips curled gruesomely, he shuddered for a bit, exhaled, and went as limp as a wet rag. Gradually his bloody hands slipped from his chest and hit the floor with muted thuds.

Rising, Fargo sought a blanket and draped it over the body. He reclaimed the Sharps and stepped outside for some fresh air. A full moon was rising, peering over the eastern rim of the earth like a gigantic yellow eye. He leaned on a post and mentally cursed himself for being as dumb as they came. For someone who wanted to help the farmers, he was doing more harm than good. Despite his help, Tom Baxter was leaving, and now Ed Morris was dead on account of him. He might be doing the rest a favor if he just rode off and left them to fend for themselves. But he couldn't. Not yet.

A shovel and a pick were stored in a small room in the stable. Fargo dug a grave near the corral and gave Morris a proper burial. By rights Laurel and Allyson should have been the ones to do it, but Fargo didn't care to leave the body lying in the house for hours on end. There was no telling when Laurel would return, if she did, and Allyson would be better off at the Walkers' where Samantha and Maggy could comfort her.

Climbing on the Ovaro, Fargo clucked the pinto forward. As he did, he spied the glimmer of reflected moonlight in a nearby field. Since he was in the shadow of the sod house, he doubted anyone had a clear shot at him. Taking no chances, though, he veered behind the house and in a wide loop that resulted in his approaching the field from the east.

Fargo tied the stallion to a bush and padded along a cornfield until he saw a horse tethered ahead. Beyond the animal a man was creeping toward the house, his spurs jingling lightly. Fargo increased his speed, passed close to the horse, a black bay he had seen once before, and stealthily overtook the visitor, coming up on him as the man reached the end of the corral. "That will be far enough, friend," Fargo said, pressing the barrel of his Colt against the man's spine.

A jerk of the shoulders was the man's only reaction. He kept his head and didn't try to draw and spin as so many would have done. "Damn, you're good," he remarked. "No wonder Rascomb doesn't want to tangle with you."

"Turn around," Fargo ordered. "Slowly."

"Like a turtle," the youngest of Rascomb's gang said. Holding his hands out from his waist, he rotated, his grin and the ivory handles on his Colt both pale contrasts to the darkness. "Go easy on that trigger, Fargo. I don't aim to die until I've got enough gray hair to make a mop."

"You know who I am?"

"Hell, everyone west of the Mississippi has heard of the Trailsman. You're as famous as Carson and Boone combined. And from the way you Indianed up on me, I reckon your rep is deserved." The young gunman chuckled. "Rascomb was fit to be tied when he found out. Ranted and raved for hours. He claimed we should head on back to Omaha and get five or six more men, but Crane pointed out what would happen if he did so he changed his mind."

"Talkative gent, aren't you?" Fargo said.

"My one failing," the gunman said, and laughed. "My pa always said if I didn't learn to hobble my lip, I'd wear my mouth out by the time I was forty. But I still got twenty-two years to go yet and my jawbone ain't showing any sign of wear and tear."

Fargo found himself liking the youngster despite their being adversaries. "What do they call you? Windy?"

"Jake Larn, at your service."

"At Rascomb's service, you mean."

"Maybe. Maybe not. To be honest, I've about had my fill of the man. And this job isn't quite like he told me it would be when he hired me." Larn sighed. "That's life though, isn't it? Chock full of surprises and not half of them the kind you'd go looking for if you was in your right mind."

"I can see what your father meant," Fargo said, lowering the Colt but keeping it trained on the gunman.

Larn snickered. "I suppose my mouth would have gotten me in over my head long ago if it wasn't for the fact I'm a heap faster with my talkin' iron than I am with my tongue."

"That's hard to believe."

"It's the truth, though. I've never met my match yet."

"No matter how fast you think you are, there's always someone faster somewhere," Fargo said.

"Do tell. But they say *you've* never been beat. And you've rubbed out more gents than Crockett did at the Alamo."

"I've been awful lucky."

"I hope I have me the same kind of luck," Larn said affably. "For some reason some hombres just take a dislike to me at first sight and have to try their hand. So far they've all come up short." He stared at Fargo's pistol. "So what's it going to be? Are you fixing to bore my belly or can I lower my arms? My elbows are getting tired."

"I don't know yet," Fargo said. "What are you doing here? Looking for me?"

"No."

"Convince me."

"It's sort of personal."

"So is being dry-gulched. And I'm sick and tired of being a target for everyone in this territory."

The gunman fidgeted, shot a glance at the house, and scowled. "I don't ordinarily advertise private matters, but I'll make an exception on your account." He lowered his voice. "I'm here to do me some courting."

"You can do better than that."

"Why would I lie? Haven't you met Allyson Morris? Now there's a gal who knows what she likes and who ain't shy about going after it, neither. The first time I saw her, it was like being a kid again and seeing the sweet candy in the jars at the general store. Made my mouth water so much I feared I'd drown."

Surprise was piling on top of surprise. Fargo had learned long ago to depend on his gut instincts, and his instincts told him the gunman was telling the truth. "You think she feels the same way about you?"

"I know she does," Larn declared. "Why, a few night ago she took me to the moon and back again. I've plumb near lost my head over that gal." He studied Fargo a moment. "Now I've been honest with you. How about you doing the same? What are you doing here? Laying for me?"

"I just killed Ed Morris."

For a full ten seconds there was silence. Then Larn cleared

his throat. "Correct me if I'm off the track, but ain't you supposed to be on *their* side?"

"I am."

"Do you make a habit of killing your friends, or was this a special occasion?"

"It was an accident," Fargo said. Suddenly he felt tired, extremely tired, and he wearily slid the Colt into its scabbard. "Larn, I'm not in the habit of giving advice unless someone asks. But I'm letting you know for your own good that you should point that bay of yours any direction you want and keep on going until the Platte is nothing but a memory. The bloodshed has just started."

"I appreciate the concern, but I'm too pigheaded to do anything but what I want to do. And I want to see Allyson again." The gunman tilted his hat at a rakish angle. "Besides, she might need some comforting and I'm just the man to dry her tears. Every woman needs a knight in shining armor."

Fargo was in the act of wheeling. He paused and regarded the younger man intently. "Maybe it's something in the air."

"What?"

"Never mind. It's your life to waste as you please," Fargo said. "Follow me." He strode to the Ovaro, waited for Larn to join him, and rode directly into the rising moon. The young gunman said nothing, but Fargo could feel Larn's eyes on him now and then. When the lights of the Walker farm blossomed in the night, he slowed to a walk. "This is as far as you go."

"Let me guess. You want me to stand watch over the crops so crows don't eat them down to the roots."

"No, you nitwit. Allyson is staying with the Walkers."

"You're going to send her out to me?"

"If I'm right, she'll come of her own accord," Fargo said. "See you around." A flick of the reins and Fargo galloped the rest of the way. They heard him coming. All four rushed out to meet him, Samantha and Allyson in the forefront.

"Skye!" Samantha exclaimed happily. "We were becoming worried. Did you find the one who shot at you?"

"Yep," Fargo said, avoiding Allyson's gaze as he climbed down. He would rather have battled a war party of Comanches empty-handed than do what he had to do next, but there was no other choice. Squaring his shoulders, he faced them and

77

something in his expression silenced them as effectively as if he had shouted at the top of his lungs. Tersely he told them everything; about seeing Laurel, about the confrontation, about Ed's unnecessary death. Everything except his encounter with Jake Larn.

A terrible quiet ensued when Fargo finished. The Walkers were in shock. Allyson Morris at first was as white as chalk. Then her jaw twitched, her fists clenched, fire sparkled in her eyes, and without warning she hurled herself at Fargo and tried to punch him in the face.

Fargo caught her arms and effortlessly held her from him while she cursed him with every profane word she knew. When she realized she couldn't hurt him with her fists, she lashed out with her feet, trying to kick his shins. Several of her kicks landed, lancing his legs with pain.

Samantha and Maggy came out of their shock. Trying to calm Allyson, each grabbed one of her arms and pulled her from Fargo.

"Take a hold on yourself, girl!" Maggy urged. "It was an accident. You heard Skye."

"You think I believe him?" Allyson stormed, flicking a foot at Fargo's groin but missing. "He murdered my pa on purpose!"

"Why would he do such a thing?" Samantha asked through clenched teeth. She was barely able to keep a grip on her incensed friend. "You're talking nonsense."

"Am I?" Allyson screamed. With an enraged wrench she succeeded in tearing loose and leaped to the right. "You don't know all that I know!" she yelled, tears pouring from her eyes. "He must have found out."

"Found out what?" Bill Walker asked. "Tell us the truth, young lady? What is going on here? Why did your mother do what she did?"

Allyson was slowly backing away, her whole body shaking in uncontrollable volcanic fury. "Damn all of you!" she hissed, jabbing a finger at the Walkers. "How can you believe him? After all the time we've been friends, you take his side! Go to hell!" Before anyone could stop her, she whirled and sped off.

"Ally!" Samantha cried, springing in pursuit. She had only taken a step when Fargo grabbed her arm.

"Let her go."

"What? Why? She's my friend and she needs me."

"She's better off by herself right now."

"No!" Samantha objected, and would have gone on anyway had her mother not taken her other arm and pulled her toward the door. "I should go after her. Please, Ma."

"Hush, child."

The moment the women were inside, Bill closed the door and said, "What the hell does all this mean? I thought I knew the Morrises pretty well, but now I guess I didn't." He ran a hand through his hair in exasperation. "I never told my wife or daughter, but I've never much liked Laurel. She was always a bit too loose around the men to suit me." He lowered his voice. "Once she even had the gall to invite me to meet her in the woods, but I made it clear I wasn't about to betray my Maggy's trust."

"She gave me the same sort of invite," Fargo revealed.

"Maybe that's why she tried to shoot you. Out of spite."

"Did she try to shoot you when you turned her down?" Fargo shook his head. "No. There was more to it than that, but I'm damned if I know what it was."

"So what do we do now?"

"Tomorrow I tell the others at the social and we take it from there."

"Solter and Jenkins will have fits. They've both been toying with the idea of leaving ever since they were beaten by Rascomb's men, but Morris and I were always able to convince them to try and ride things out. This will change everything. They might head East right away with Baxter." Walker sagged against the wall. "And I don't mind admitting I'm sunk if they do. Maggy and Samantha won't want to stay if we're the only ones left. And I can't blame them. There'd be no one else around to help us in a fight, no one to visit with, no socials, no way to break the boredom. I'd be through." He stared out over his farm. "All the time I've spent, all my work, would count for nothing."

"I'll do what I can to help you," Fargo said, "but Solter and Jenkins might not think too highly of me after they hear about Morris."

"You never know. I think they knew about Laurel. It wouldn't surprise me if she threw herself at both of them, too. Anything in britches is fair game to that woman." Bill paused. "Where do you figure she went?"

"I thought it might be here," Fargo answered, listening to loud sobs coming from within. "It sounds like your family needs you. I'll be in later." Snatching the pinto's reins, he headed for the stable. Mechanically he went through the motions of watering and feeding the Ovaro and giving the stallion a rubdown. In no hurry to have to answer more questions from the Walkers, he took his time, hoping they would soon turn in. The lamps were still lit when he was done, so he walked to the hay and sat down on a soft pile, then stretched out his full length and pulled his hat over his eyes.

Instantly Fargo was asleep. He dreamed about a gigantic creature dressed like Laurel Morris but with the face and claws of Nightmare pouncing on him in the dark and ripping him to pieces. Vaguely he became aware of a hand on his chest. In his confused state he thought it was the paw of the creature attacking him and he grabbed it and sat up.

"Skye. It's me, Samantha. You're hurting me."

Feeling leaden, his senses numb, Fargo blinked at her crouched beside him. She had on her nightgown and heavy robe and was trying to tug her hand from his grasp. "Sorry," he blurted, letting go.

Samantha rubbed her hand while studying him. "Are you all right?"

"Fine."

"Why haven't you come in yet? Are you going to sleep out here all night?"

"Why not?" Fargo said, lying back down. He propped his head in his hands and stared at the beams overhead, wishing she would go and leave him in peace. "What are you doing out here? You should hustle your rump inside before your folks get mad."

"They're both sound asleep. Have been for over an hour." Samantha slid close to him and rested on an elbow. "I couldn't sleep no matter how hard I tried."

"So you came out here to talk," Fargo said testily.

"Not exactly."

Fargo, curious, looked at her just as her soft lips descended on his mouth.

8

Skye Fargo was about to give Samantha Walker a light push and to tell her to quit bothering him when her silken tongue caressed his own and her full breasts ground into his chest. His loins twitched, and despite his wish to be alone he felt himself responding to the seductive pressure and the warmth of her nicely contoured body. Absently he brought a hand up to stroke her hair while his other hand stroked her spine from her neck to her hips.

Samantha milked the kiss for all she could, lingering over him as her hands roamed over his powerful chest and stomach. On raising her head, she exhaled and grinned. "Has anyone ever told you that you are a champion kisser?"

"Not lately," Fargo said.

"Mind if I help myself to seconds?"

"Treat yourself to as many helpings as you want."

Tittering, Samantha kissed his face, his brow, and his throat. She licked his earlobe, then nibbled on his skin as if he were an ear of corn and she was famished. Her left hand, meanwhile, circled around and around his groin, never quite inching close enough to touch it but serving to arouse Fargo to a slowly building fever pitch nonetheless.

Fargo let her do as she pleased. This was her first time and he wanted her to enjoy it to the fullest. He rubbed her back, massaged her buttocks, and kneaded her thighs. Gradually she became more and more excited, as demonstrated by her heavy breathing and the plaintive cooing sounds she made. Her hips began to thrust into him of their own accord and her breasts strained against her nightgown.

The heavy robe was discarded first. Then Fargo hiked her nightgown so he could savor the glassy surface of her inner thighs and stoke the fires smoldering in the depths of her womanhood. Samantha tossed her head back and moaned. When his finger probed into her, she arched her back and dug her nails into his arms.

Fargo was in no rush. He spent the longest time playing with her breasts and slowly pumping his finger in and out of her moist inferno. She languidly moved her body and her sighs rose in volume, becoming panted gasps. Eyes closed, she was relishing every tingle, every thrill.

Fargo felt she was ready for the next step. Unbuckling his gunbelt, he pulled his pants down. On seeing his large penis, she tensed and started to draw back. He took her hand and gently placed it on himself, prompting her to shudder and lick her lips.

"You're so huge. I had no idea."

Fargo kissed her. She made no attempt to remove her hand. Instead, she began stroking him, her touch so exquisite it nearly drove him over the brink of self-control. For someone who had no experience, she knew exactly what to do. Nature took over where reason faltered and in short order she had him quivering with rampant desire.

Next Samantha loosened his buckskin shirt so she could run her eager hands over his bare flesh from his neck to his knees. She giggled every so often, like a little girl reveling in a new toy she had just been given. And she couldn't get enough of him. She explored every nook and cranny, going so far as to delve the tip of her tongue into his navel.

Fargo lowered her onto her back, enfolded a hard nipple in his mouth, and sucked. Her arms looped about his neck, pulling him closer. Her legs wrapped around his midsection, her heels locking onto his posterior. She was as ready as she would ever be, as primed as any woman ever had been. Yet still Fargo refrained from joining completely. He knew that those pleasures longest denied were the most intense, so he held her in a state of anxious suspense for minutes on end.

There came a time when Fargo sensed he should make his move. Parting her legs wider, he touched his organ to her opening, paused when she stiffened, and fed himself into her a fraction of an inch at a time. Her eyes widened in amazement. She clutched at him as if drowning. When he was all the way

83

in, she trembled and groaned and swayed her hips back and forth.

"Hang on," Fargo said softly. Rocking on his knees, he resorted to the age-old rhythm of lovemaking. At the apex of each thrust Samantha cried out, inarticulate sounds that meant nothing and everything. At the outset she was too nervous to do more than cling to him, but as he continued to stroke and the friction sparked a wildfire within her, she met his thrusts with counterthrusts, the vigor of her motion matching the rising tempo of her passion. Their bellies slapped together, their mouths were glued tight.

Fargo planned for her to crest first, but he had a difficult time holding himself back. A familiar sensation at the base of his manhood told him he was on the verge of spurting and he ground his teeth together and tried to last a few more minutes. Then Samantha woke every animal in the stable with her moans and he felt her gushing so he held on to her hips and gushed, too, pounding into her in a frenzy.

Later, as they lay side by side with Samantha's head resting on Fargo's shoulder, she ran a fingernail down his chest and snickered.

"If I'd only known."

"Ummmmmm," was all Fargo could think to say.

"I should have done this years ago, but I had no idea what I was missing. Ma raised me to be a good girl and good girls don't do things like this."

"We live and learn."

Samantha shifted to peck him on the chin. "I'm glad I waited, though. You were very gentle, very sweet. You made it very special for me."

"Glad to oblige," Fargo said.

"Was it this wonderful for you the first time?"

"Must have been. I can't seem to get enough."

Laughing, Samantha nuzzled him, touched his manhood, and asked, "Didn't you say I could have as many helpings as I want?"

"Again? So soon?"

"What's wrong? Did I wear you out?"

Fargo could have told her the truth. He could have said he was simply too tired after all he had been through the past few days, with scant rest and food, to boot, and he needed to catch up on his sleep. But he didn't. He saw the hungry appeal in her eyes and he said the one thing that would satisfy her and have her smiling secretly to herself for years to come. "You wore me to a frazzle. No woman has ever made love to me like you just did."

Surprise gave way to joy on her face. Samantha sat up, giggled, and gave him a slap on the behind. "Well now. That's about the nicest thing anyone has ever told me. And here I figured I might not be much good at it."

"You're the best," Fargo said. He draped an arm over his mouth to hide his grin as she hurriedly dressed, lowering it when she bent down to give him one last kiss.

"Coming in soon?"

"Maybe," Fargo said. "But don't wait up."

"Don't worry. I'll sleep like a log tonight." Samantha flung her arms out and spun merrily in a circle. "I feel so happy! Do you know the feeling?" Without awaiting a reply, she skipped to the door, puckered her lips at him, and vanished.

"Me and Sir Galahad," Fargo said to himself, his eyelids drooping. He managed to muster enough energy to don his pants and his shirt, then he sank back down and drifted into peaceful slumber.

What awakened him Fargo couldn't say, but suddenly he had his eyes open and was looking around for the source of a noise he thought he had heard. The lantern had burned low. Through the parted door he could see the sky was still dark, but there were streaks of light to the east that indicated dawn would soon arrive.

Twisting, Fargo glanced to his left, then froze. Jake Larn stood a few yards away, that fancy ivory-handled Colt in his right hand and trained on Fargo. Larn's left arm was tucked against his side.

"Morning."

Fargo slowly sat up. His own Colt was close but not close enough for him to grab it before the young gunman fired. "This is a hell of a note," he complained. "I thought you'd give me a fighting chance."

"I would, if I was here to gun you down," Larn said, his mouth curling downward. "But I'm not."

"You could have fooled me," Fargo said, nodding at the six-shooter.

"I just didn't know what kind of reception to expect," Larn said, advancing a pace. He seemed to wince, then he grunted and went on. "These nesters ain't none too fond of anyone who works for Rascomb. Or used to."

"You've quit him?"

"I haven't had time to tell him to his ugly face yet, but I was thinking about it before I met you. Back in Omaha, Rascomb claimed these farmers were in the wrong, armed to the teeth, and as mean as riled rattlers, but they're a harmless bunch who couldn't hold off a few Sioux squaws. I don't like killing folks who don't have a prayer against me." Larn took a pace. "Our talk made me see that more than ever. If a man like you sides with these squatters, then Rascomb has been lying to us somewhere along the line."

Although Fargo was itching to reach for his Colt, he sat perfectly still, uncertain whether he could trust the gunman not to fire. "I didn't count on seeing you again for a while," he remarked. "Didn't Allyson and you get together last night?"

"We did," Larn said, his gun arm sagging. "She about ran smack into my horse, she was so mad. I took her home and had to listen to her rant and rave about how she's going to see you die in the worst way she can think of. In case you don't know, she's a mighty feisty woman when she sets her mind to something."

"I have a fair notion of what she's like."

Larn looked down in disgust at his gun hand, muttered under his breath, and dropped the Colt into his holster. "You think you do. I know I thought I did until we had our fight." He grinned and pressed a palm to his forehead.

Fargo noticed beads of sweat on the gunman's brow, which was odd since the air was so cool. Standing, he picked up his revolver. "You look as if you need some rest. Why don't you stick around and join us for breakfast? The Walkers will be happy to have you if you've changed sides."

"Have you ever made an idiot of yourself, Trailsman?"

"Once or twice. Why?"

"Me, too. Usually a woman's involved. There was the time I trusted a dove in St. Louis with my money poke and she ran off to New York City with it. Never did find her again. Seems to me I would have learned then and there, but no. Later I took the word of another dove that she loved me and set up house for her with furniture and curtains and everything, and darned if I didn't come home one day and find her in bed with a drummer. A lousy drummer. Proved she had no taste at all."

"Are you talking to hear your own voice or do these stories of yours have a point?"

"The point is I can't be blamed for believing Allyson loved me when she claimed she truly cared. After the things we did, I thought I'd found the woman of my dreams. I was half set to marry the bitch."

"What did she do to wake you to the truth?"

"We had a fight, like I said. She insisted I shoot you for killing her pa. Said it would prove my love and she'd be mine forever." Larn snorted. "I wanted to please her more than anything, but I told her I couldn't do it. For one thing, considering her temper, if I went around shooting everyone she doesn't cotton to, I'd spend a fortune on shells. For another, I sort of like you."

"How did she take it?" Fargo asked.

Larn made a clucking sound. "Not very well at all. The damn hellion shot me." So saying, he moved his left arm, revealing a wide red stain on his shirt. Suddenly his eyes fluttered, his legs buckled, and he pitched over.

Fargo barely got his arms under Larn in time to keep the gabby gunman from hitting the ground like a downed tree. "You are an idiot," he declared, carefully lowering Larn onto his back. A quick check showed the bullet hole was in the fleshy area to the left of the rib cage. By tilting Larn, Fargo located the exit wound. From the angle, Fargo judged the heart and other vital organs had been spared, but Larn had bled a great deal.

Somewhere a strident jay was greeting the new day as Fargo dashed to the house. He knocked loudly, entered, and had a pot of water on the stove when Bill and Maggy Walker stumbled from their beds.

"What's all the ruckus about?" Bill wanted to know.

A short explanation sufficed to get Maggy boiling the water and Bill tearing an old sheet into strips to use as bandages.

"Samantha!" Maggy called. "We need your help." She looked at Fargo. "Sometimes I think that girl would sleep through the Second Coming. I don't know what gets into her."

Fargo knew, but he wasn't about to enlighten the parents. Returning to the stable, he waited at Larn's side until the family joined him. Maggy knew just what to do. As with most frontier women, she'd tended her share of work injuries and wounds. Fargo was shooed aside so the bullet hole could be dressed. Then Fargo and Bill placed Larn on a board and carried the gunman into the house where he was deposited on blankets in the corner opposite from Fargo's.

Samantha said little. She couldn't take her eyes off Larn from the moment she first saw him and hovered over him every minute.

Once everything settled down, Maggy made breakfast. She had to work hard to keep the flapjacks coming, as Fargo was famished. Eight flapjacks covered with syrup, four biscuits, six eggs, and five cups of coffee later he pushed back from the table and excused himself.

"You're not leaving us again?" Bill inquired.

"I'll be at the Morris place. Laurel might have come back by now, and Allyson has to answer for shooting our young friend."

"Be careful, Skye. Those women are sheer poison."

Fargo swung to the northwest once the house came into sight and approached on foot through the high grass. With the Sharps cocked, he ran to the corner, verified there was no commotion inside, and crept to the door, which hung open.

Someone had ransacked the place. Silverware, dishes, clothes, towels, and other articles were scattered over every square inch of the floor. Chairs had been upended. Pillows had been slashed apart. All six drawers in a dresser had been yanked out and the contents spilled.

Since the culprit was long gone, he was going to head for the Walker farm when he remembered Morris's stock. A check of the barn turned up four horses and three cows. He couldn't very well leave them there or they might share the grisly fate of Baxter's animals, nor could he turn them loose to fend for themselves. He was standing in the entrance, mulling over what to do, when riders appeared. They were half a mile to the southwest. Fargo suspected they were Rascomb's gang. He climbed into the loft to surprise them.

The surprise was on Fargo. There were eight in the party, consisting of Baxter, Solter, and Jenkins and their wives, plus Solter's young son and Jenkins' ten-year-old daughter, all on their way to the social. They halted in front of the house and Tom Baxter called for Ed to come on out.

"Ed Morris is dead," Fargo announced from his perch.

The whole party wheeled around in alarm, the men unlimbering their rifles, the women and children moving to the rear. When they saw who it was, they relaxed a little.

"What was that you said?" Solter declared anxiously. "What's happened to Ed? Where are Laurel and Allyson?"

Fargo indicated the fresh mound of earth in the shadow of the corral. "I buried Morris myself," he answered, and did not elaborate. He knew they would pester him with countless questions and some might not believe him. In his opinion it would be smarter to wait until they were all at the Walker farm where he had friends who would back him up. With that in mind, he climbed down the ladder and joined the group. Several of them started to talk at once and he silenced them with a gesture. "Now is not the time. Everything will be explained at Bill's." He nodded at the stable. "For now, it's important we do something about Ed's stock. We can't leave them here unguarded."

"What do you suggest?" Tom Baxter asked.

"That we take all the animals to the Walker place. When all of you are together you can decide what to do with them."

The suggestion met with unanimous approval. So, with the horses and cows herded in tow, they traveled swiftly to their destination. Once there, everyone crammed into the house and Bill Walker related the details of Ed's death. Raised eyebrows and suspicious looks were shot at Fargo when Bill told about Ed falling on the meat cleaver, but no one challenged Fargo's version of the events.

Fargo left the house so they could talk freely among themselves. He leaned on a post, debating whether to stay for the social or to track down Rascomb and get to the bottom of the mystery. Staring off at the Platte, he saw a lone horseman bearing down on the farm at a trot. The immense size of the man in the saddle left no doubt as to the horseman's identity.

Gar made no attempt to hide the dislike in his beady eyes as he reined up and dismounted. "You," he said scornfully. "Gar was hoping you would not be here."

"Someone has to make sure you behave yourself."

The giant sneered. "So the puny man thinks he can keep Gar in line? Huh! The big protector of Ally and Miss Sam."

"Allyson won't be here today," Fargo divulged.

"Where is she?"

"How should I know?"

The news appeared to unduly agitate the trapper. Gar bit his lower lip, rubbed his calloused hands together, and looked off to the southeast. Suddenly glancing at Fargo, he turned to his horse and took down a string of four dead rabbits. "For the stew," he said, waving them. "Gar always does his part."

"Caught any beaver lately?"

"Not for several days," Gar answered. He lifted a ponderous foot to the porch, then stopped, his expression darkening. "Was that you, puny man? Were you the one who sprung two of Gar's traps?"

At that moment the door opened and out stepped Samantha. She tensed on seeing the giant but forced a smile. "Why, hello Gar. I should have known you would make it."

"For the pot," Gar said, extending the rabbits.

"Would you take them in and give them to my mother?" Samantha requested sweetly.

Gar hesitated, his narrowed eyes on Fargo.

"Please," Samantha insisted, laying a hand on the giant's arm. "It would be so nice of you. Mother will want to get them on the stove right away."

Glowering resentfully, the giant shuffled indoors.

Samantha started across the yard. "Walk with me, Skye. I need to know some things."

Fargo fell into step behind her. "Such as?"

"This Jake Larn. What can you tell me about him?"

"Not much."

"I mean, he must be a bad man if he rides with Rascomb, but he's so polite when he talks to me and so considerate and all, I can't hardly believe he's a vicious gunman like the rest of that gang."

"He's come around?"

"Three or four times, yet never for very long. Infection has set in. It's not serious, but he has a fever and he won't be on his feet for a couple of days." Samantha kicked at a small stone. "He'll need a lot of nursing until he fully recovers. Ma doesn't have the time, so I guess it's up to me. I'm just not certain I want to."

"Why not?"

"He's our enemy, isn't he?"

"Not anymore. He's decided to quit Rascomb."

"He has?" Samantha brightened. "Well, in that case I suppose it's my duty to do what I can to restore him to full health. I mean, it's no different than nursing a sick critter."

"No different," Fargo said, finding it hard to maintain a straight face. "And he's bound to be grateful. The two of you might wind up close friends."

"That would be nice," Samantha said almost too casually. She touched Fargo's hand. "Before I forget, I want to thank you again for last night. That meant a lot to me. It's made me see things differently. There is a lot more to relationships than I realized. What we did isn't necessarily the evil some folks claim."

"I've never thought so," Fargo said. They were close to the stable and Samantha stopped in the entrance.

"How strange life can be," she said. "There's so much I don't know about, so much I haven't experienced. Living on a farm is nice, but it's so sheltered. I want to see more of the world. Do you think that's wrong of me?"

"I'm not the one to say. No one but you can decide what's best for you."

"I know. But—"

Samantha suddenly gasped. Fargo saw that she was looking over her shoulder in barely concealed terror an instant before a heavy, steely hand clamped onto the back of his neck and squeezed so hard he thought his spine would crack.

"We're not done yet, puny man. Gar wants some words with you."

9

So quickly did Gar strike that Skye Fargo had no chance to defend himself. He lifted a hand to try and grasp the vise holding his neck and was sent stumbling into the stable by a brutal shove that drove him to his hands and knees. Fargo pushed upright, or tried to, and was spinning to face the giant when a battering ram struck him on the shoulder and knocked him flat.

"What's wrong, puny man?" Gar asked, standing with his massive hands on his thick hips. "Have you had too much to drink? Is that why you can't stand on your own two feet." He cackled at his jest.

"Leave Skye alone!" Samantha said from the doorway. "He's done nothing to you."

"Wrong, Miss Sam," Gar said. "This weakling has been making trouble for Gar from the day he came here. Gar is tired of it."

Fargo was slowly standing. Dazed by the last blow, he longed to plant a fist in the giant's smirking face but feared he was too rattled to connect. His shoulder ached abominably, his neck was sore. He clenched his right fist, holding it ready at his side so the trapper couldn't see it.

"There will be no fighting on our property," Samantha told Gar. "Pa will throw you off if you don't behave."

The threat caused the giant to ponder for a few seconds. "It would be worth it," he then declared, and abruptly swung a granite fist. For one so big, he was extraordinarily fast, his bulging sinews more than compensating for his bulk.

Fargo would have been knocked unconscious if he had not been expecting just such a move. By a fraction he ducked under the blow, which caught his hat instead of his face, and, pivoting, he delivered a punch to Gar's groin. The giant gurgled and retreated a step. Pressing the advantage, Fargo closed and swung a two-punch combination to Gar's stomach. It was like beating on an iron skillet.

The ineffective blows allowed Gar to catch his breath. Roaring like a berserk animal, he snapped a right jab that missed and followed through with a left uppercut that didn't.

To Fargo, a hammer seemed to clip the tip of his chin and he was catapulted rearward to land, stunned, in the hay pile. Had the hay not cushioned the impact the fight would have ended then and there. But Fargo was able to rise and meet the next attack, sidestepping as Gar tried to grasp him in a bear hug. A kidney punch straightened Gar, another crumpled him against a stall.

Gar's tremendous constitution enabled him to rebound immediately. Snarling, he lashed an arm backward, catching Fargo in the chest. Fargo went down, flat on his back. Gar, taking a short step, leaped high into the air and came down with both of his heavy boots leveled to smash Fargo to a pulp.

"Skye!" Samantha screamed.

Fargo rolled, and kept on rolling. He heard the loud thud of Gar landing and felt something clutch at his shirt. Then he pushed to his knees and twisted. Gar was after him. A boot the size of his head swept at his face. By throwing himself to the left Fargo evaded it.

"Gar! Stop!"

The giant treated Samantha as if she wasn't there. Beside himself with fury, he sprang.

A skip to the right spared Fargo from being crushed to the ground. For a moment the trapper's side was exposed and Fargo threw a pair of straight rights to the body that jarred Gar and made him retreat a step.

Setting himself in an awkward boxing stance, Gar waded in.

Fargo braced his legs and met the giant head on. Knuckles skimmed his ear. In retaliation he flicked a series of jabs, but all he accomplished was to bruise his hands on Gar's jaw. A fist fanned his cheek. Fargo tried a right cross, a sharp, stunning blow that seldom failed to drop a foe. Gar blinked, sneered, and attempted to clinch.

Too savvy to let himself be caught, Fargo back-pedaled. He glimpsed Samantha rushing from the stable, no doubt for help, then had to concentrate as Gar lunged. Fargo parried several blows, each swing costing him in pain and more bruises. He had never fought anyone so nearly indestructible and he was at a loss as to how he could prevail.

Gar sensed the indecision. "What's wrong, puny man?" he snapped, stopping. "Is Gar more than you can handle?"

"You wish," Fargo replied. Like a human whipcord he swung again, throwing everything he had, all of his strength and weight, into an uppercut. He thought his hand would break when he scored.

Taken off guard, Gar tottered. Blood flowed from his lower lip. He shook his head to clear it and held his arms in front of his body to protect his face and stomach.

Since Fargo couldn't go high, he went low. Hitting below the belt wasn't tolerated in public boxing bouts, but this was a fight for his very life. He drove a punch deep into Gar an inch above the groin, and when Gar lowered his arms, Fargo snapped the back of his elbow into the trapper's cheek, splitting the skin.

"You hurt Gar!" the giant thundered. Fists on high, he charged, heedless of his vulnerable body.

Fargo had no recourse but to dart out of the way of those twin sledges. In his haste, however, he failed to note a nearby stall and ran right into it. Anguish sheared his left knee. Limping, he tried to put more distance between the giant and himself, but Gar had seen his mistake and wasn't about to let him recover.

Saliva and blood dripping from his parted lips, the trapper imitated a bull running amuck and simply lowered his head and attacked.

Fargo tried to jump from harm's way. His hurt knee couldn't take the pressure and his leg buckled, causing him to sag. He brought his arms up a second before the giant plowed into him. In a whirl of limbs they both went down, Fargo to end up on his back with Gar lying across his chest.

Whooping in triumph, Gar sat up and straddled his enemy. "Now, puny man," he gloated, "Gar teach you to tamper with Gar's traps."

Trying to push the giant off was akin to heaving off a mountain. Fargo bucked and strained and accomplished nothing. He was helpless, about to be pounded senseless or worse. Sunlight streaming through the entrance highlighted Gar's right fist as Gar slowly raised it.

"That will be quite enough!"

Gar froze.

Fargo had to crane his neck to see Bill Walker and the other farmers clustered in the doorway. Behind them were the women and children.

"You heard me, Gar," Bill Walker said. "Get off Fargo and stop this nonsense this minute."

"Go away. This is Gar's business."

"Not when it's on my property," Bill held his ground. "My daughter tells me that you started this so I'm holding you and you alone accountable. Unless you want to be thrown off my farm, you'll do as I want."

"Gar is tired of being told what to do," the trapper said. "Everyone thinks Gar is so stupid, but Gar isn't." He reached down, seized Fargo by the throat, and rose, hauling Fargo with him. "But Gar will do as you want. Gar will not fight on your property." He grinned wickedly. "Gar will take puny man off your property so Gar can end this once and for all."

"You'll not take Fargo anywhere," Bill said.

"Watch," Gar said.

Fargo was dragged forward, his heels scraping the dirt. Vainly he tried to break the giant's grip. He wasn't about to let Gar take him and his right hand dropped to the Colt. Only the Colt wasn't where it should be; during the fight the six-gun had fallen out of his holster.

The farmers and their families backed up as Gar advanced. They parted, permitting Gar to move past them toward his horse. All of them, that is, except Samantha, who put herself in front of him.

"Stop!" she cried. "Listen to reason, Gar. If you do this thing, I will never talk to you again."

"Out of Gar's way, Miss Sam."

"Not until you drop Skye."

"Skye, is it?" Gar gave Fargo a rough shake. "You like this tricky bastard. Gar can tell. But Gar will not put him down, not even for you."

"Haven't I always treated you as a friend?" Samantha asked, resting a hand on the trapper's stout wrist.

"Yes," Gar begrudgingly admitted.

"Have I ever been rude to you? Or refused to talk to you?"

"No."

"Then for my sake, if for no other reason, let go."

Fargo had been inching his hand lower and lower during the discussion. His fingers touched the top of his boot and he was slipping them under to grip the hilt of the Arkansas toothpick when Gar unexpectedly gripped him in both hands and shook him harder than ever, so violently his teeth rattled.

"Gar will not!" the giant raged. "This means more than you can know. Gar is sorry." Brushing Samantha aside as easily as a normal man might brush aside an annoying gnat, Gar took several more strides, then stopped short when the blast of a revolver shattered the air.

Fargo, hanging low to the earth, blinked and coughed when the slug kicked dirt in his eyes and mouth. Glancing around, he saw who had fired and grinned.

Jake Larn, his chest heavily bandaged, was framed in the doorway to the sod house. In his right hand was his fancy Colt, smoke curling from the barrel. He had on just his pants. Swaying slightly, he stepped next to a post and coughed. "That's far enough, you bush ape."

"This does not concern you, boy," Gar said harshly.

"I beg to differ. That's my new pard you're toting around like so much dirty linen. I'd take it kindly if you'd set him down and go find a grizzly to mate with or whatever you do to amuse yourself."

"You're making a mistake."

"I've made them before," Larn said. Suddenly his eyes drooped and he sagged against the post, but only for a bit. His jaw twitching, he uncoiled and cocked the Colt. "I'm not going to waste my breath jawing with you, you big ox. You might think that if you stand there long enough I'll keel over and you can go on your way, and you could be right. I do feel poorly. But before I hit the ground I can promise you that all four pills in this wheel will be in your head." Larn smiled, an extremely painful smile. "Care to see if I'm a man of my word?"

Gar was a study in frustration. He glanced at Fargo, then at the young gunman. "Gar knows how good you shoot. Gar knows you mean what you say."

"Then you'll have to settle with Fargo another day."

Being released was like being shot from a cannon. Fargo was slammed onto the ground with such force he heard bells ringing in his skull. The hammering of hoofs soon drowned out the bells, and hands under his back supported him as he sat up.

"Are you all right?" Samantha asked.

"Other than feeling as if I was stomped by a buffalo, I'm fine," Fargo answered. He spotted Gar galloping madly away and said softly, "Soon, you son of a bitch. Real soon."

"Wasn't Jake wonderful?" Samantha said. "He saved your life. Feverish and ailing, he left his bed to help you."

"Shucks, ma'am," Larn said. "It wasn't much. Now if you'll excuse me." He tried to turn, to go inside, but his feet became entangled and he toppled against the post.

"Jake!" Samantha cried, forgetting all about Fargo as she dashed to the gunman's aid and steadied him before he could fall. Looping an arm under his, she guided him through the doorway.

Fargo slowly rose and dusted himself off. The farmers converged on him, wanting to know if he was injured. He assured them that he wasn't, then entered the stable and searched for his Colt, which he found under the hay. Blowing dust off the cylinder, he emerged to discover the men bringing the table outdoors for the social. Chairs were set up. One of the women produced a pitcher of cold tea, another laid out a thick pie, and Maggy added a plate piled high with sweetmeats. While the children played with a wooden hoop, Bill Walker brought a fiddle out and tuned it playing snatches of various songs. The incident with Gar was all but forgotten. This was the weekly social and the farmers would let nothing stand in the way of their having a grand time.

Fargo worked his way into the house. Jake and Samantha were the sole occupants, with Jake propped on a pillow and Samantha feeding him from a soup bowl. "I wanted to thank you," Fargo said.

"What for? I saw you reaching for your boot. What's down •

97

there? A derringer or a blade?" Larn asked, and continued without waiting for a response. "Another minute, I expect, and you would have taught him that size don't count when the other fellow is in the right and keeps on coming."

"How are you holding up?"

Samantha was the one who answered. "He'll do fine if he'll just stay in bed and quit doing so much darn talking. I've never met a man so in love with his own voice."

"He wore out my ears, too," Fargo said. The lively twang of the fiddle started him for the door, but Larn called out.

"Wait, Fargo. I've got something important to say."

"It can wait," Samantha said.

"No, it can't." Larn flinched as he attempted to sit up. "It's about Rascomb."

"I'm all ears," Fargo said.

"He was planning something for today. I don't rightly know what, 'cause he never let us know his plans ahead of time. But he did say that the day of the next social would be the day he earned his five hundred dollars."

"Someone is paying him to drive the farmers off?"

"Yep. Didn't you know? Rascomb takes his orders from someone in Omaha. I never met the boss myself, but Crane did and Crane claimed we were working for a mighty important person, someone with a lot of clout in high circles. I tried to learn more but I couldn't."

Fargo remembered Walker telling him that Rascomb made regular trips to Omaha. Now he had an inkling why. "Why does the man who hired Rascomb want this strip of land so badly? Hell, he's got practically all of the Nebraska Territory to choose from."

"Only Rascomb knows and he ain't saying. He did let it slip once that a heap of money is involved. A heap."

"I don't see how," Fargo confessed. Since the federal government hadn't opened the territory to settlement yet, by rights the land was almost worthless. Even if the man in Omaha drove the farmers off, what good would it do him? There was no one the man could sell it to because other farmers would rather take up unclaimed land than pay for acreage. The whole business was loco. "You take it easy, Jake, and I'll see you later."

"One more thing," Larn said. "It's about Crane."

"The tall one?"

"Yep. He's been fuming ever since you gave him that toss. Says he'll rub you out personally."

"I've been threatened before."

"By many gents who own a needle-gun?"

"What's a needle-gun?" Samantha asked.

"An old kind of rifle," Larn said. "Buffalo hunters used them a lot 'cause of their stopping power and their range."

Which, Fargo reflected, was four hundred yards or more in the hands of a skilled marksman. While not quite a match for his Sharps, the needle-gun would enable Crane to safely pick him off from so far away that the first and only warning Fargo would have would be when the bullet ripped through his body. He didn't like it one bit. "I appreciate the warning," he said.

"Figured you would." Larn settled back down, making himself comfortable, and beamed at Samantha. "Never thought I'd live to see the day that talking wore me out, but it does." He nodded at the bowl. "To get my strength back, I reckon I'll need a lot more of that delicious soup of yours. It's about the best I ever ate."

"I just threw it together from scraps and such," Samantha responded, clearly tickled by the compliment. "One of these days you'll have to try my cherry pie. It will make your mouth tingle."

"I can hardly wait," Larn said softly.

Fargo had to leave before their cow-eyed shenanigans made him lose control and he hurt their feelings by laughing himself to tears. The farmers and their families were having a fine time, with the adults dancing to a lively tune while the young boy and girl clapped and urged them on. None of them noticed him as he went by.

It took a couple of minutes to saddle the Ovaro. Instead of swinging to the left when he went out the door and riding past the homesteaders, he turned to the right, took the corner of the stable at a trot, and brought the pinto to a gallop once he was in the open.

Despite the ever-present danger from Crane and the needle-gun, he made straight across the open prairie to the Morris house, which was still deserted, and from there to the Solter farm. Fargo was worried about Rascomb. If the hired killer had boasted that this day would be the day he earned his pay, then Rascomb must have a scheme that would put a permanent end to the fond dreams of the farmers. And there was only one thing Fargo could think of that would have the desired effect.

All was quiet at the Solter place. The same with the Jenkins'. He hesitated, thinking that Rascomb wouldn't bother the Baxter spread because Baxter had already announced his intention to leave. But then he realized Rascomb had no way of knowing that, so he rode all the way to the last farm. He felt he had wasted his time when he got there and found all was well.

Dismounting, Fargo led the Ovaro to the water trough and stood by while the stallion drank. He removed his hat to wipe his brow, and as his gaze drifted to the northeast he stiffened on seeing a group of riders approaching. Yanking on the reins, he hurried the stallion into the stable and pulled the door almost all the way shut, leaving enough space for him to peek out.

All of the dead animals had been removed, but the pale stench of blood hung in the air and there were stains where the pools had dried. The Ovaro sniffed and snorted, disliking the scent of death, and Fargo had to calm the horse down with a few words and soothing strokes before he could attend to the matter at hand.

Rascomb and company circled the farm before venturing close. Then they fanned out, rifles shucked, and converged at a walk. Rascomb, Fargo noticed, hung the farthest back. A skinny gunman, at Rascomb's command, rode in first and made a sweep of the yard and the corral.

"All clear," he shouted.

A smug smirk showed that Rascomb believed he had completely outfoxed the farmers. As he slowed to a stop he glanced at his companions and said, "See? What did I tell you? They're too stupid to post guards. Every last squatter is at the social, so there's no one to stop us."

"I don't mind tellin' you," said a stocky rider, "I don't much go for all this sneakin' around. If you're goin' to kill a man, up and do it, I always say."

"Did I ask for your advice, Hays?" Rascomb said.

"No. I'm offerin' it free," the stocky gunman refused to be

cowed. "I was hired because I'm right handy with a pistol. We all were. And you said we'd have plenty of chances to use our guns. But that hasn't been the case. All we've done is beat up a couple of stupid nesters and spent the rest of our time spyin' on them. Hell, you could have hired my kid sister to handle this bunch."

"I'm getting sick and tired of all the griping," Rascomb said. "First that wet-nosed Larn and now you."

"Funny. I never heard you call him that to his face," Hays remarked. "And I think Jake had a point. This ain't no fight for a grown man. If things don't change I just might pull my freight."

Rascomb jabbed a finger at the gunman. "I wouldn't, if I was you. That wouldn't make the boss very happy. He expects you to fulfill your end of the deal, and if you don't, he might send someone to set you straight."

Fargo, Colt in hand, could have leaped out and taken them by surprise, but he hesitated, hoping he would learn the identity of the man behind the war on the homesteaders.

"Let him try," Hays said with a gruff laugh. "I don't scare easy."

"You would if you knew who it was." This from Crane, the tall killer carrying the needle-gun. "Trust me, Hays. You don't want to brace him. With the pocket change he carries, he can hire a half-dozen men to come after you if he's so inclined."

"You keep tellin' us how important an hombre the boss is supposed to be," Hays said. "Why not prove it? Tell us his name?"

A few of the others muttered, apparently in agreement.

"You knew the rules when you signed on," Rascomb said. "The man who hired us wants it kept a secret. What's wrong with that? He stands to lose a hell of a lot more than any of us if the truth ever got known." He looked at another gunman. "Now enough jawing. Stinson, you and Edwards go into the house and pile everything that will burn in a great big pile. Empty the lamps on it and wait for my word to set it ablaze."

Fargo had feared as much. The gang was going to burn out each and every farmer, working their way east from the Baxter place. It was unlikely the farmers at the social, busy as they were with dancing and eating and having fun, would notice the smoke until too late. He pressed a palm to the door, about to make his presence known. Suddenly the men outside all glanced in his direction. With very good reason.

The Ovaro had just whinnied.

10

Skye Fargo clamped a hand on the pinto's muzzle to prevent the horse from whinnying again, but the harm had already been done.

"I thought you said all the stock had been killed?" one of the gunmen commented.

"All except two horses and a single cow," Rascomb said. "And Baxter should have taken the horses to the social. Stinson, go have a look-see."

Fargo heard the jangling of spurs. He had nowhere to hide the stallion and no way to escape other than out the front, where the killers clustered. Striding to the door, he swung it outward a few more inches while showing himself in the opening. "Howdy, gents," he declared. "I hear tell you're out for my blood."

The hardcases gaped. Stinson, only a few yards from the stable, was the first to regain his senses. Cursing, he clawed at the revolver on his left hip. Two shots boomed and he tottered backward, clutching at twin holes high on his chest. Wordlessly, he toppled.

Fargo saw the rest coming to life, saw five guns swinging toward him, and threw himself to the right with not a heartbeat to spare. A ragged volley rang out. The edge of the door splintered and shattered as round after round punched holes through the wood. Huddling at the base of the wall, Fargo waited for a lull for the rash killers to empty their weapons. Then, bounding to the opening, he snapped off an answering shot.

The hired guns were seeking cover. Rascomb and Crane were racing behind the corral. Another man was almost to the house. The last killer was darting toward the northwest corner of the stable. This was the man Fargo's slug hit, catching him a few inches above the waist. The gunman spun and fell. However, not fatally wounded, he scrambled to his hands and knees and reached the safety of the corner.

Fargo pivoted to shoot at the man nearing the house, but he had to duck back when Rascomb and Crane opened up from the corral. Three shots were all they fired, enough to keep him pinned down while the other man sought cover. When next Fargo peeked out, none of them were in sight.

So much for the element of surprise! Fargo reflected. Now his enemies had the upper hand, and in light of how devious they were, he was certain they'd devise a means of flushing him out so they could finish him off. And they would not have to be in any great hurry, either. The farmers would be busy all day at the social; Baxter and his family probably wouldn't get back until late that night.

Fargo glanced at the closed rear door. The first thing the killers would do was surround the stable to trap him. If he hurried, he might be able to flee out the back before they did. But the door wasn't big enough for the stallion to pass through, and he wasn't about to leave his horse behind to be stolen or shot to pieces.

The only other means of entering or leaving was through the small hayloft at the front, just like in the Walker stable. It seemed that all of them had been built according to the same design. Fargo ran to the ladder to climb up, then changed his mind and sprinted to the rear door instead. He hoped to secure it to prevent any of the gunmen from sneaking inside when he was otherwise occupied, but there was no bolt to throw, no bar to set in place. Country folk were trusting souls, too trusting for their own good sometimes.

So Fargo improvised. He stacked four bales of straw beside the door. The bales wouldn't keep anyone out, but they would slow down whoever entered and give him time to welcome them with lead. Jogging to the ladder, he reached the loft and inched to the small hay doors. The right-hand door was ajar enough for him to see the corral and part of the house. He saw two horses at the far end of the former, the mounts belonging to Rascomb and Crane, but not the killers themselves. A shadow flitted across the window in the house, indicating someone was up to something in there.

Fargo tried to imagine what the killers would do next. Burning him out was the most likely step. To do so they had to get near enough to the stable to set it ablaze, which would be easy enough to do on either side where he had no way of holding them at bay.

Resigned to waiting for them to make the first move, Fargo sank onto his stomach. A board a foot above his head abruptly exploded inward, while without a cannon blasted. In reflex, he pressed his face to the floor and held an arm over his head as splinters rained down. He didn't need to be told to know who had fired—Crane, using the needle-gun.

"Hey, Trailsman!" the tall killer shouted gleefully. "If I missed, why don't you step on out here and I'll part your hair for you."

The taunt had come from the corral. Fargo crawled to the left, thinking a different angle would permit him to spot the braggart, but he saw no one. And the breeze had already dispersed the puff of gunsmoke so he couldn't pinpoint Crane's position that way.

Rascomb added his two bits' worth. "Fargo? Can you hear me? I want you to know your death will be talked about for years. I aim to skin you, make a pouch out of your stinking hide, and show it everywhere I go!"

The voice, Fargo deduced, came from the house. Rascomb had moved. Digging his elbows in, Fargo cautiously backed to the ladder and descended. He looked about, racking his brain for a way out of his fix. In one of the stalls stood the sole cow, munching contentedly on hay. There was a spare saddle and some blankets adorning a rail and farm implements leaning in a corner. Over to one side was a plow. By it sat a small wagon.

A brainstorm brought Fargo to the wagon. Bits of grass, pieces of hay, and clods of dry manure littered the bed. He lifted the tongue, testing its weight. Then, hardly straining at the effort, he hauled the wagon over and aligned it in front of the great door, making a point to leave the tongue jutting upward against the body of the wagon so it wouldn't drag when the time came to implement his plan. Gathering hay to fill the bed required a few more minutes.

A faint scratching noise at the side of the stable lured Fargo on silent feet to the wall. Without, there was whispering and the clink of metal against the hard ground. The hired guns were up to something. Smiling, he quickly retrieved the Sharps, inserted a cartridge, and glued an ear to the wall until he felt fairly certain he knew where the two killers were crouched. Then, leveling the rifle, he fired.

A startled yelp attended the retort. Boots thumped, receding swiftly, while a man fumed a blue streak and another kept saying, "My leg! My leg!"

Reloading the Sharps, Fargo stepped to the wagon. He lined up the Ovaro behind it, slid the rifle into the boot, and opened a saddlebag to remove his flint and steel. Since he spent so much of his time in the wild, he rarely had matches on hand for starting fires and did so using the time-honored technique employed by every mountain man since the days of Lewis and Clark. By striking the steel on the flint, he caused sparks to shoot off, which in turn lit suitable punk, or tinder, and kindled a roaring blaze. In this instance he lit the hay itself, and by fanning the tiny flames produced with his breath he set the contents of the wagon to burning.

Now Fargo had to work rapidly. He stuffed the flint and steel in the saddlebag, dashed to the great door, and impatiently bided his time as the crackling flames rose higher and higher. With them came clouds of white smoke, so thick he could hardly see the pinto. At the proper moment, he shoved the door with all his might and darted behind the wagon. Scooping up armfuls of loose hay, he dumped them on top of the burning hay in the bed, which increased the amount of smoke fourfold.

There were shouts outside. A single gun spoke.

Throwing his shoulder against the rear of the wagon, Fargo dug in his heels and pushed. The burning hay was so close to his head that his face broke out in a sweat. Sheets of flame danced within inches of his hat. He could feel the intense heat through the tailgate as he put all of his weight into forcing the wagon to move forward. It did, but only a few inches. For some reason the wheels wouldn't turn freely. Fargo tried harder, gritting his teeth, his powerful shoulder muscles bunching.

The wagon lumbered into motion, rattling out the opening and into broad daylight. So much smoke was now pouring out that a gray cloud enveloped the entire front of the stable. None of the gunmen could see inside.

Fargo raced to the Ovaro, swung up, and worked his legs. The pinto leaped for the entrance, skirting the wagon on the right. Another volley rang out as Fargo bent low and hung on the off side of the pinto, Indian fashion. Blinding, acrid smoke covered him for several seconds, then he was in the clear and galloping past the corral. Guns thundered inside the house.

The ruse had worked. Fargo was out and unharmed and sweeping around the end of the corral when a tall figure popped up not three yards off. He recognized Crane, recognized the needle-gun the killer was bringing to bear, and since he couldn't hope to outrun a bullet, he resorted to the only tactic left; straightening, he reined the stallion sharply to the left and rode straight into the gunman.

Crane's eyes widened and he took a hasty bead, but he had yet to level the long barrel of his rifle when the Ovaro slammed into him. The pinto's chest struck him full on the torso as the needle-gun cracked, the shot going wild. Yelping, Crane was flung into the corral as if hurled from a slingshot. Two of the upper rails cracked and Crane fell through them, winding up upside down with his legs caught in the lower rail.

Fargo never allowed the Ovaro to break stride. Galloping past the corral, he sped into the open. Two guns opened up in the house, one at the door, one at the window. Neither of the killers drew blood. Seconds later he was past the house and flying for his life toward the cottonwoods and willows bordering the Platte River.

Fargo didn't expect pursuit. At least two of the gunmen were hurt, and Crane might well be dead. Working the reins to lash the stallion on, he covered a hundred yards or more when a lone rifle cut loose behind him. Going back to the old Sioux trick of riding on the side of his mount, he plunged into a field of high grass. Soon the shots tapered off.

The sanctuary of the trees gave Fargo a breather. Halting, he twisted in the saddle but saw no one after him. They were too busy with their wounded, he reasoned. And since they believed he was gone, the last thing they would expect would be for him to take the fight to them. But that was exactly what he intended to do.

Fargo circled to the west. Leaving the stallion in a stand of saplings, he grabbed the Sharps and worked his way through the fields until he had an unobstructed view of the front of the house and the corral. He saw a man helping another to a horse. None of the others were in sight and he feared they might be preparing their indoor bonfire. Making himself comfortable, he sat and rested his elbows on his knees. The wind was blowing at his back so he need not adjust his sights for windage. Nor was the elevation a factor. All he had to do was take deliberate aim, and when the wounded gunman was perched in the saddle, Fargo stroked the trigger. The instant the rifle banged, he began reloading.

Arms flapping, the paid killer toppled. The other gunman spun, drew his pistol, and fanned several wasted shots as he dashed into the house.

Now there was a temporary lull. Fargo had them pinned in the house. There was no rear door, no way out other than by the front door or the window if they so chose. And when they came out, he'd be ready. Lowering his hat brim to ward off the glare of the sun, he fixed the front sight on the dark doorway. There might be three men left, perhaps only two. Not enough to give the farmers cause to worry, and in a short while they would have even less cause.

When Fargo observed two of the horses moving, he didn't think much of it. Then he realized the horses were drifting toward the house. He saw their heads uplifted, their ears perked, and guessed why. The killers must be quietly beckoning the mounts closer so they could dash out and make their escape. One of the animals lowered its head under the narrow wooden overhang that had been attached to the front of the sod roof to afford shade in the daytime, and the following moment Rascomb appeared, coming through the doorway with his fingers clutching at the reins.

Fargo had Rascomb square in his sights for all of one second. His finger was tightening on the trigger when the other gunman dived through the window, directly into the line of fire. The Sharps blasted, bucking into his shoulder, and the gunman jerked around in midair, bent nearly double, and dropped like a rock. Rascomb, untouched, vaulted onto his animal.

Replacing the spent cartridge took virtually no time, yet it was enough for Rascomb to wheel his horse and gallop to the southeast. Fargo cocked the hammer, raised the Sharps, and was just fixing a bead on Rascomb when the stable came between them. "No," he fumed. Rising, he ran to the south, expecting to see Rascomb again once he had a clear view beyond the stable, but he caught only a glimpse of the panicked weasel. Rascomb had veered eastward. Fargo tried to line Rascomb up in his sights again but was unable to do so.

Unwilling to accept defeat, Fargo ran toward the buildings. If he could reach the corral before Rascomb vanished, he still might end the bloodshed. But when he sped past the stable there was no one on the open prairie. At the corral he stopped and rested the Sharps on the top rail. Rascomb had to be out there somewhere! he assured himself. But where?

"Don't move, you son of a bitch!"

Fargo might have tempted fate had not a shuffling sound alerted him that the gunman was only a few yards behind him. He stayed still as the shuffling drew nearer.

"Drop the rifle and turn. I want you to see it coming."

The speaker was the gunman hit while diving through the window. A spreading red stain marked his flannel shirt and there was a nasty welt on his temple.

"You must have a lot of sand," Fargo said. "A Sharps can drop an elk in its tracks."

"Keep your mouth shut," the gunman said coldly. "Just unbuckle your gunbelt and let it drop. Then step away."

Resorting to slow movements in order not to give the killer an excuse to fire, Fargo did exactly as he had been directed. The step he took was to the right.

Rascomb's man relaxed. "You plugged me clean through, you bastard, but you missed my vitals. Which is too bad for you." He chuckled, or tried to, and coughed instead. "Wait until Rascomb hears it was me who rubbed you out! I'll get extra for this."

"They won't pay you a cent," Fargo said.

"I told you to keep your damn mouth closed!" The gunman took a faltering stride and coughed some more. "All I want is to see the look in your eyes when I shoot, to see the fear on your face when you breathe your last." Another pace brought him that much closer. "I like watching others die, Trailsman. Always have. Men, women, kids, it's never made any difference."

Fargo mentally measured the distance between them.

"I think I'll start with one of your knees and work my way up," the gunman said. Lifting his six-gun, he went to take precise aim.

Desperation drove Fargo to take a lunatic gamble. He had no way to avoid being shot. Reaching the killer before the man fired was impossible. Unless Fargo could somehow divert the man's attention for the crucial moment it would take Fargo to make a single leap, he would die. So it was that he resorted to the oldest ruse known, a trick invented before Fargo was ever born. He glanced past the gunman, over the wounded man's shoulder, and let his eyes go wide as if in surprise while he also grinned in mock relief and declared, "Don't shoot, Baxter! Maybe we can take him alive."

The killer took the bait. In his wounded state perhaps he wasn't thinking clearly. Or perhaps he really believed that Baxter might not have gone to the social and had helped lay an ambush for the gang. In any event, the man pivoted to see who was behind him.

Fargo sprang, his arms extended, and was almost upon the gunman when the man awoke to his mistake and spun. The six-gun swung toward Fargo's head, but Fargo batted it aside with a wrist. Then Fargo rammed into the killer and they both tumbled, the Trailsman sliding a hand inside of his right boot as he fell. The Arkansas toothpick flashed in the sunshine.

Hacking and sputtering, the gunman rose to his knees first but was slow in raising his revolver. Fargo threw himself at the man's chest, the toothpick glistening as the razor sharp blade cleaved the space between them and then sliced into flesh and sinew. Fargo knew exactly where to bury the knife to puncture the heart. The gunman went rigid, whined, and gaped at the hilt sticking from his body. His six-gun was forgotten as he feebly tried to tug the blade out. Failing in that, he looked blankly at Fargo and said "I'll be damned!"

Skye Fargo slowly stood. He glanced at the first man he had shot, insuring the man was dead, then at the paid killer he had shot off the horse. Both were motionless, their vacant eyes locked on the blue sky. But Crane, and Crane's horse, were gone. Fargo had no idea when the tall killer had fled, if indeed Crane had. Rascomb was the only member of the bunch Fargo had seen ride off.

Taking nothing for granted, Fargo crouched down to strap on his gunbelt. He also stayed low as he picked up the Sharps and crossed to the house. Cocking the rifle, he stealthily neared the doorway. A peek showed the pile of possessions the gunmen had started to make in the center of the floor. A chair had been overturned, too, but the rest of the furniture was where it should be.

The house turned out to be empty. Next Fargo checked the stable, where the cow was still chewing its cud, oblivious to all that had gone on.

By now the hay in the wagon had burned itself out and the wagon itself was ablaze, giving off thick brown smoke. Fargo saw sparks blowing toward the stable. Rushing inside, he grabbed a pitchfork and applied the tines to the tail end of the wagon. The heat wasn't quite as intense, but he had to work harder than he had earlier to push the wagon far enough from the stable to prevent any random sparks from setting the structure alight. Afterward, Fargo dragged the three bodies to the nearest tilled field and buried them. He didn't want any of the farmers coming on rotting corpses. It was the middle of the afternoon when he hiked to the Ovaro and headed for the Walker farm, and when he arrived the families were just sitting down to an early supper.

"We wondered where you got to," Bill Walker said as he motioned Fargo to a chair. "Have any trouble today?"

The food was forgotten as Fargo recounted the clash at the Baxters'. Tom Baxter was fit to be tied and wanted to ride straight home, but the others convinced him to stay until the social was over. After calming down, Baxter wrung Fargo's hand and thanked him over and over for saving his property.

"Too bad you're fixing to leave it all behind," Fargo mentioned.

"Not anymore," Baxter said. "While you were gone we had a talk and it was agreed that we'd divide up the Morris stock and I could have all I need to replace the animals killed by Nightmare." His eyes watered in gratitude as he gazed at his friends. "It's a new lease on life for me and mine and I can never make it up to any of you."

Walker glanced at Fargo. "It won't be like we're stealing the animals. We're all pitching in what we can, and between the four of us we have enough to pay Laurel and Allyson fair value for the critters." He paused. "That is, if we ever see them again."

"Where do you suppose they got to?" Mrs. Solter asked.

"You don't think that vile Rascomb got his hands on them, do you?" Maggy wondered.

Fargo had been puzzling over the same thing. He doubted the women had decided to head back East alone. They lacked the supplies needed to reach the settlements, not would it be wise for a pair of women to travel that far without protection. "I aim to try and find them in the morning," he said.

"Be on the watch for Rascomb and Crane, too," Bill said.

"Hell, they're gone by now," Tom Baxter said. "The two of them together don't amount to a hill of beans. They know they're licked and they won't bother us again."

"You hope." Bill disagreed.

Fargo ate heartily. There were venison steaks, potatoes, thick loaves of piping hot bread, and corn on the cob. Delicious pie was the dessert. His belly was full to busting when he took the stallion to the stable and bedded it down for the night. Not long afterward the other families departed.

"You coming in?" Bill Walker asked. "I have a set of checkers if you'd care to play a game."

"No thanks," Fargo responded. He thought of Samantha and Jake Larn. "I need to turn in. And if you don't mind, I'll sleep in the stable again tonight."

"Whatever you want," Bill said, grinning.

Fargo spread his blankets out on a layer of hay, propped his saddle to use for a pillow, and lay down with a grateful sigh. The darkness and quiet were comforting after the hectic events of the day and he was lulled to sleep within minutes. But it seemed he had hardly closed his eyes when he opened them again and held himself still, listening. He couldn't say how he knew, but he was certain someone else was in the stable with him.

The pad of stalking feet confirmed he was right.

11

Fargo's hand closed on his Colt as he raised his head to survey the center aisle. The great door was closed and there was no hint of movement in its vicinity. Twisting, he glanced at the rear door, which had also been shut when he fell asleep but which now hung partway open. Slinking along between the stalls was a low, tawny shape, and as it came abreast of a stall occupied by a cow, it stopped and moved toward the animal.

In the gloom details were difficult to discern. Fargo could make out the inky silhouette of a feline form, but the outline wasn't quite right. The body was too bulky. And the tail, instead of twitching in feral anticipation, hung limp, dragging on the ground.

Fargo carefully pulled his pistol and muffled the click of the hammer by covering it with his other hand. The stalker paused, its head swinging around as the huge body rose a few inches higher. So far the intruder was unaware of Fargo's presence, but he knew it would soon spot him lying there. With a quick flip he was on his stomach, taking aim.

Displaying speed that belied its size, the creature whirled and streaked like an arrow toward the rear door. Fargo had seen Nightmare close up, had witnessed for himself the big cat's graceful movements. In contrast, the thing before him was like an ungainly bear, waddling clumsily but swiftly. Fargo banged off two shots, and at the second blast the stalker fairly flew at the door and smashed it aside.

Fargo sprinted after the thing. A cool wind caressed his skin as he dashed outdoors. He swung to both sides but failed to find the stalker. Nor could he see it in the grass. On a hunch he ran to the southwest corner and was rewarded by spying a vague form barreling across the field. He clasped the Colt in both hands, aimed, and fired once.

The stalker was swallowed by the earth.

Fargo lowered his six-shooter and removed the spent cartridges as he mulled over continuing the chase. He had a fair notion as to what—or who—he had seen, and he wasn't about to confront the party responsible until circumstances were more to his liking. Only a fool rushed off across the prairie after an enemy in the middle of the night. He could afford to wait until a few more questions were answered to his satisfaction.

Excited shouts had broken out at the house. Fargo's name was being shouted repeatedly. Lantern light lit the interior as he walked into the stable and latched the door behind him.

"Fargo!" Bill Walker cried, coming down the aisle. "Are you hurt? We heard shots?"

"What happened?" Samantha asked.

"We had a visitor," Fargo disclosed, choosing to add, "It looked like Nightmare."

"That stinking mountain lion!" Bill said. "Isn't there no satisfying that beast? After what it did to Baxter's stock, you'd think it would have had its share of blood for a spell."

"Cougars have to eat, too," Fargo commented.

"How can you say such a thing? You know how much our horses and cows mean to us. Without them our farms can't prosper."

"Don't get your britches in an uproar," Fargo said. "Things aren't as they seem. I'm not so sure Nightmare is to blame for the dead stock."

"Are you saying there are two mountain lions?" Maggy inquired.

"No, ma'am," Fargo said, "not anymore, but there had to be at one time."

"You've lost us," Bill said.

Fargo sank down on his blankets. "I'll explain everything once I know for sure. In the meantime, don't kill Nightmare unless you see the cat going after one of your animals."

The farmer shook his head in amazement. "Do you know what you're asking?"

"Yes."

114

Bill lowered the lantern and gazed at the horses and cows in the stalls. "I've trusted you this far so I reckon I'll go the distance, but it makes me nervous to think of that cougar prowling around as it damn well pleases." He stared at the rear door. "How did it get in here, anyhow?"

"Came in through the back," Fargo said.

"Tarnation! Wasn't the door latched?"

"It was."

"Then how in the world did the mountain lion get inside? Cougars can't open doors."

"Makes you think some, doesn't it?" Fargo responded as he lowered onto his back.

Bill Walker's eyebrows puckered and he thoughtfully chewed on his lower lip. "Well, I'll be," he said at length. "If you're right, that puts a new slant on everything."

Fargo nodded. "Spread the word. The others should be warned so they can take precautions." He draped his hat over his eyes. "And don't look for me at breakfast. I'll be getting an early start."

True to his word, Fargo was up an hour before dawn and riding to the southeast. The eastern horizon was blushing pink and birds were already warbling in the trees along the river. Fargo chewed on a piece of jerky, the only meal he was likely to get all day. Until the sun came up he didn't bother hunting cover, but once it did he utilized what little there was.

Over a mile from the farm Fargo came on horse tracks made within the past twenty-four hours, a pair of shod mounts that had moved side by side. He stuck to them for the better part of two hours, until well after sunrise. The farms, the Platte, the hills, the rutted Oregon Trail itself, had all fallen far behind him when a break in the prairie materialized in the distance, a gap that broadened out into a narrow ravine create by erosion. The tracks led down into the ravine.

Fargo climbed down and walked along the rim. He had gone only a few dozen feet when a tendril of smoke advertised the location of those he was after. Walking rather than riding, he returned to the mouth of the ravine and slowly negotiated a steep incline that brought him to the ravine floor, which was wider than it had appeared from the rim and covered in spots with brush. Fargo secreted the pinto, then, palming the Colt, advanced vigilantly until he saw where the smoke was coming from.

A spacious shelf had been carved out at the base of the right-hand wall. At least ten feet deep, thirty feet wide, and eight feet high, it was an ideal shelter against the elements. Close by, a pool of water reflected some of the sun's rays.

A spring, Fargo figured, and he had to admire the layout. From here Rascomb's men could reach any of the farms within half a day. And only if someone stumbled on the site, or could track as well as he did, were they liable to be discovered. He snaked nearer through the brush. Four horses came into sight, all grazing by the spring.

Fargo saw someone seated under the shelf by the fire. It was a man, but Fargo couldn't tell who it was because the figure was facing away from him. Avoiding a dry twig, he drew ever closer, and he was to a point where he could almost see the man's profile when an unexpected threat stopped him cold.

"Drop the hog-leg or die. It's your choice."

The voice was Crane's. Fargo had no doubt the gunman had the needle-gun pointed at his back, and he was wise enough to foresee the outcome if he attempted to spin and fire first. So, offering no objections, he did exactly as he had been told.

"Damn. I was hoping you'd be stupid." Crane sounded genuinely disappointed. "Now hoist your arms, you bastard."

Fargo did, and was shoved so roughly he tripped and fell to his knees. He began to turn, but a gun barrel poked into the base of his spine.

"Clumsy, Trailsman. Real clumsy. Get up and try again."

Swallowing his anger, Fargo obeyed. He hiked his arms and walked toward the shelf. The man at the fire swiveled, gawked, and rose grinning in triumph.

"As I live and breathe! Skye Fargo. You should have let us know you were coming and we'd have put more coffee on." Rascomb tittered, his hands on his hips. "Where did you find him, Crane?"

"Sneaking through the brush." The tall gunman came around to stand to one side. He had picked up Fargo's Colt and wedged the revolver under his belt. A wicked gash scarred his face, running from his chin to the corner of his left eye. "The idiot must have thought we wouldn't be smart enough to post a lookout."

"And just when I was beginning to think all my luck had gone sour on me," Rascomb said. "With you out of the way, our troubles are over. We'll have those nesters dancing to our tune in no time."

"Let me do it here and now," Crane said. "I owe him for this." He placed a finger on the gash and glared at Fargo. "You about broke my neck when your horse plowed into me."

"I'll try harder next time," Fargo said.

"There won't be a next time," Crane responded angrily. Whipping the rifle high, he took a step, intending to bash the stock into Fargo's head.

"No!" Rascomb barked. "Not yet. After all the harm he's done us, let's do it right." Rascomb swiveled to stare at the deep shadows at the rear of the shelf where a number of blankets were partially visible. "Besides, our lady friends would be upset if we didn't let them know we have a visitor." He raised his voice. "Rise and shine, you lazy bitches! I swear, if you ever get out of the sack before noon, the shock will kill me."

Fargo watched a pair of slender shapes rise out of the shadows and stroll toward him. He shouldn't have been taken aback, but he was, a little. "Fancy meeting you two here," he said.

Laurel and Allyson Morris were rubbing sleep from their eyes and patting their hair into place. Neither registered the slightest surprise.

"Well, well, well," the redhead said. "You finally caught him, Rascomb? What did he do? Walk in and surrender?"

Allyson sashayed up to Fargo, flaunting herself, her hips swaying suggestively. "Hi, lover. How have you been? Did you miss me?"

An answer was on the tip of Fargo's tongue. Suddenly he was pushed to one side and Crane towered over Allyson, his features contorted in rage.

"Him, *too*? Isn't there a man in these parts who hasn't seen you bare-assed, you lousy whore?"

"I'm not no whore," Allyson bristled. "I've never taken money for my favors in my life." She smirked. "And come to think of it, yes, there were a couple of fools who turned me

117

down." She stroked the stubble on Crane's chin. "Not that it should matter to you. I'm yours now, sweetheart. Quit being so bothered by the past."

Crane seized her wrist and twisted, prompting a squeal of pain. "You'd better remember you're mine when we get to Omaha. Try running out on me, woman, and I'll turn you black-and-blue when I find you."

With the tall killer distracted, Fargo saw his chance, or thought he did, and he took a quick step, grasping at the needle-gun to wrest it from Crane's grasp. But a brutal blow to the back of his skull felled him before he could lay a finger on the rifle, and he pitched forward. The ground leaped up to meet his face. Then everything faded to black as somewhere someone cackled.

The oddest sensation brought Fargo around. He felt a strange prickling on his neck, as if something was being rubbed up and down across his skin. Senses swimming, he struggled to clear his head. He involuntarily groaned and the scraping stopped.

"At last! You had me worried, handsome. I thought Rascomb hit you so hard you'd never rejoin the living."

Fargo cracked his eyes and grimaced as torment stabbed through his head. Licking his lips, he looked up into the laughing eyes of Laurel Morris. She was smiling sweetly.

"Don't try to move. It will only make it worse."

Not understanding what she meant, Fargo tried to raise an arm but couldn't. He looked to his right and learned his wrist had been tightly bound to a stake driven firmly into the earth. All his limbs had received the same treatment and he was now staked out, Indian style, a few yards from the fire. "What's this?" he asked through dry lips. "Are they going to torture me first?"

"Rascomb mentioned something about making a pouch from your hide when he has the time," Laurel said. She rubbed a fingernail across his neck. "Such a waste! A healthy specimen like you should be put to better use."

"Where are they?" Fargo asked, searching the shelf. "And where's Allyson?"

"All gone, handsome," Laurel answered. "Rascomb has a plan to force Bill Walker to leave and Allyson is part of that plan. It's quite clever. For the life of me I can't imagine how he came up with it. In any event, they won't be back until nightfall." The tip of her tongue flicked out her parted lips. "Maybe a lot later. We have the whole day to ourselves."

"Rascomb left you to guard me?"

"Don't sound so surprised. That fool and I have an agreement. In exchange for letting him fondle me under the covers, he's agreed to see me safely to Omaha." Laurel leaned back and gave the ravine a look of contempt. "I can hardly wait to be back in civilization. The biggest mistake I ever made was marrying that dumb hick Ed."

"He loved you."

"I know. Which is why I tried to make our marriage work for the first couple of years, until he dragged me out into the middle of this godforsaken prairie. I couldn't take the loneliness and the boredom any longer. I told him I wanted to give up the farm and live in a city, any city, but he wouldn't agree."

"The two of you were only married a few years? Then Allyson was his stepdaughter."

"That she was. The poor girl hated farm life more than I did, but somehow she managed to make the most of it."

"By bedding everything in pants," Fargo said. "You must be proud of the way she took after you. Does she aim to be a madam one day, too?" His mouth had no more closed than he was struck, a ringing slap to the jaw that cracked his teeth together and drew drops of blood from the corner of his lower lip.

"Be civil, Trailsman," Laurel hissed. "Rascomb wants you alive, but he didn't say you had to be in one piece." She shifted, reached behind her, and produced the Arkansas toothpick. "He left this pigsticker he found when he was tying you, and your Colt, for me to use. And use them I will if you speak ill of my daughter again."

Fargo couldn't take his eyes off the knife. There went his best hope of freeing himself. He'd hoped to somehow loosen an arm so he could get to his boot; he hadn't known the gunmen had found the toothpick.

"We shouldn't be squabbling when we can spend the time

in a much more pleasant manner," Laurel continued. "You be nice to me and I'll make a point of being nice to you."

"Like you were when you tried to bushwhack me?"

"I was afraid you'd kill Rascomb and spoil my only chance at escaping this miserable life," Laurel said. "I'd been planning for some time to leave Ed, but I didn't know how to go about it until Rascomb showed up. One day he and his men came on me when I was out riding. They tried scaring me by forcing themselves on me, but when Rascomb saw how much I liked it, he developed a personal interest in my welfare. We made our pact, if you will. And since I don't want anything to happen to him before he gets me safe and sound to Omaha, I took matters into my own hands."

"Did your husband know about you and Rascomb?"

"I think he suspected. He started being very suspicious about my long rides toward the end there. But he never made an issue of it. He was too nice a person for that."

"And look at what it got him," Fargo remarked.

"I see that look in your eyes. Don't blame me for Ed's death. If he had done as I wanted and gone back to civilization, everything would have worked out dandy. He was too stubborn, though. He insisted I'd accept our life here if I'd give it a little more time." Laurel snorted. "The jackass!"

Fargo had to turn away so his disgust would not be apparent. He thought of Rascomb and Crane and Allyson on their way to the Walker farm and wished there was something he could do to thwart their scheme. Being helpless infuriated him, and he set his mind to working on how he might turn the tables on his captors. "Any chance of my getting some water?" he asked.

"Sure. I wouldn't want you to suffer," Laurel joked. "I'll be right back." Going to where supplies were strewn loosely over the shelf floor, she snatched a tin cup up and made for the spring.

The instant the woman turned her back, Fargo went into action. Sucking air into his lungs, he tensed, then strained against the stakes, his arms and legs quivering from the exertion as he tried to tear the stakes loose. There was virtually no slack, however, and the stakes were so deeply imbedded that not one of them so much as budged. The veins on his temples bulged, his stomach muscles tightened until they resembled bunched knots, yet he couldn't loosen a single wrist or ankle. As Laurel rose from the spring, he promptly went limp so she wouldn't suspect what he had been doing.

"Here you go, handsome." Laurel squatted, held the cup to his lips, and advised, "Drink slowly so you don't spill any."

Fargo complied, aware of her eyes roving hungrily over him as he drank. The woman simply couldn't help herself. She was as addicted to men as some people were to sweets or others were to opium. The thought gave birth to inspiration and he pondered the odds of success as he finished off the water and lowered his head. "Thanks."

"Care for some food? I can whip up a plate of beans in no time."

"I wish I had an appetite. You're a fine cook," Fargo complimented her. "You proved that at your house the other night."

"Why, thank you," Laurel said, flattered. She gave the cup a dainty toss and sat so close to him her thighs nearly touched his body. "No matter what you think of me, I did do my best to please Ed at first. Not only did I learn to cook, I also got quite good at sewing and knitting." She snickered. "The girls who used to work for me would have laughed themselves silly if they saw how domesticated I became."

"What will you do once you reach Omaha? Go back to the old life?"

"I don't have any other choice. I have to earn a living and Ed didn't leave me a cent." Laurel folded her arms on her knees. "The man was a miser. He hoarded the little we had in a poke he kept hidden in the house. I went back and tried to find it but couldn't."

Fargo had his answer as to why the house had been ransacked. "That's too bad," he said, "but I wouldn't worry if I was you. Any woman as pretty as you are won't find it hard to make ends meet."

"You really think I'm pretty?" Laurel beamed and ran a hand through her hair. "I must look a sight, what with having to live in this dusty old hole until Rascomb drives the farmers off."

"You look no different now than you did at your house. I could hardly keep my eyes off you."

Laurel arched an eyebrow. "I thought you acted a bit cold toward me."

"What else could I do? Your husband was right there."

"Why, Fargo! You naughty devil!" Laurel laughed and placed a hand on his upper arm. "You sure had me fooled." Suddenly she sobered. "You couldn't have liked me all that much, though. Not after the way you slapped me around."

"Was I supposed to bring you flowers for trying to kill me?"

Peals of mirth shook the redhead. "I see your point. No, I suppose you did what I would have done if I'd been in your shoes." She gently squeezed his arm. "No wonder those slaps hurt so much. You have big muscles, big man." Her voice acquired a husky tone. "And I do so like men with lots of muscles."

Fargo had to be careful. He dared not be too obvious or she would guess the truth. "I've always liked redheads," he said casually, and looked off across the ravine. "If things had turned out differently, who knows?"

Laurel glanced at one of the stakes, then tapped a long finger on the tip of her smooth chin. "It would help to pass the time," she said softly, as if to herself.

"What would?"

"Nothing," Laurel said. Standing, she stepped to the fire and fed a few small branches to the low flames. Every so often she would look at Fargo. Presently she returned and stood over him. "Doesn't a condemned man have the right to a last request?" she asked.

"So they say."

"If you could have or do anything you wanted before Rascomb takes to carving you up, what would it be?"

Here was the moment Fargo had waited for. Devouring her with his eyes, he replied, "What do you think it would be?" Sighing, he shifted, deliberately moving his hips so her gaze would be drawn to his groin. "But we both know there's no way it can happen so why bother bringing it up?"

"Haven't you heard that old saying?" Laurel asked. "Where there's a will, there's a way." Rotating, she dashed to the rear of the shelf and came back bearing a blanket which she folded into a square. "Here. I want you to be comfortable." She slipped a palm under his head so she could lift it high enough to slide the blanket underneath him to serve as a makeshift pillow.

"What are you up to?" Fargo inquired.

"Haven't you figured it out yet?" Laurel responded. Grinning in sultry fashion, she propped her hands on either side of his head and lowered her full lips to his waiting mouth.

12

Never in Skye Fargo's life had so much depended on the effect of a single kiss. He had to stimulate Laurel Morris as he had never stimulated a woman before. He had to convince her she'd be passing up the opportunity of a lifetime if she didn't give in to her smoldering passion. So as her lips touched his he darted his tongue deep into her mouth. Her tongue met his, then followed it as he withdrew his tongue. He sucked on her as he might on a piece of fruit, savoring her silken smoothness. The redhead's full breasts pressed onto his chest and he squirmed to further arouse her. The kiss lingered and lingered.

"Oh, mercy," Laurel declared when she eventually broke for air. "You are talented." She traced a finger along his mouth. "If I let this chance pass, I'll never forgive myself."

"You can't be thinking what I think you're thinking," Fargo said, still acting a part. "I can't lift a finger to help out. You wouldn't enjoy yourself."

"Don't worry," Laurel said, lying flush against him. "Let me do all the work. I know just what to do."

Fargo responded ardently to another kiss. He felt a hand roaming over his upper chest while fingers played in his hair. Her lips moved to his neck, to his earlobe. There was no denying she had a lot of experience. She knew just how to touch him, just where he was the most sensitive. He didn't need to pretend to be excited.

"This is fun," Laurel said when, at length, she paused. "I can do as I please, and you don't have to do a thing but lie here and enjoy yourself."

"Don't stop," Fargo urged. "I'm afraid Rascomb will come back sooner than you expect and spoil everything."

"I told you he'll be gone until late." Laurel touched her

moist lips to his cheek, then to his throat. Her tongue lathered his neck as her hands tugged at his shirt, freeing it.

Fargo's mouth was smothered again. His shirt was tugged high enough for her to rub her warm palms over his body. Laurel covered every square inch, relishing his iron muscles and his flat stomach. In due course her lips strayed lower and she nibbled on his skin. Twice she bit him, hard. Her fingers kneaded his flesh. His organ stiffened, forming a bulge in his pants.

"What have we here?" Laurel asked in delight when she noticed his erection. Her left hand lightly stroked the bulge. "Lord, how huge are you?"

"See for yourself."

Like someone unwrapping a precious gift, Laurel undid his belt and his pants and hiked them down. She gasped, said "Oh," and enfolded him in her right hand. "You must be part stallion, lover."

Fargo closed his eyes when she began running her fingers the full length of his manhood. No matter what she did, he had to hold back the explosion. If he failed, his life was forfeit. But her delicate touch, combined with her hot mouth on his belly, was almost more than he could bear. He bit down on his lower lip, countering the pleasure with pain.

Suddenly Laurel switched tactics. Her mouth descended to his pole and closed on the tip.

A bolt of sensual lightning ripped upward from Fargo's groin, causing him to bite harder. He pulsed with exquisite joy. Every pore cried for release and he hovered on the brink of coming. By sheer force of will, he held himself in check, his fists clenched as he fought a silent battle with his own body.

Bit by bit, Fargo gained some measure of control. He found it helped to imagine a stone wall and to think of absolutely nothing but the wall. Laurel was devouring him with her mouth and caressing his legs and buttocks, but he was detached from the sensations she provoked.

Then Laurel abruptly stood. Lust lighting her features, she stripped off her clothes, throwing her dress and her undergarments aside as if she couldn't undress fast enough. Her sleek, velvety figure was a magnificent sight; the rounded, jutting breasts, the marble thighs, and the reddish thatch of hair at the junction of her legs. "What do you think, big man?" she asked, proudly adopting a sexy pose.

"You're beautiful," Fargo said.

"And you're terrific yourself," Laurel said, straddling him. She gripped his manhood to angle him upward and slowly sank down, aligning her body so that he knifed into her wet slit. Moist, yielding walls encased Fargo in their silken confines as he impaled her to the core. "Oh, God!" she squealed.

Fargo throbbed from head to toe. He saw her cup her hands to her breasts and commence massaging them, her forefingers tweaking the nipples. Her hips began moving, rocking back and forth and sliding up and down. It was almost too much to bear. He shut his eyes tight again and concentrated on the stone wall in his mind.

"You feel so good," Laurel said. "So damn good."

So did she, but Fargo wasn't going to admit as much. She bucked into him like a wild mare, her head thrown back, her mouth open. Panting heavily, Laurel picked up the tempo, grinding her hips as if she were a human corkscrew. She was striving to drive herself over the edge, and for the next several minutes she lost herself in her own ecstasy.

"Do me!" Laurel cried. "Pound me, lover! I want it! I want it bad!"

Now came the moment Fargo had been waiting for. Everything depended on how she reacted to what he said, which was, "I can't."

Laurel didn't hear him. "I'm almost there. Rip me apart!"

"I can't," Fargo said, louder than before.

"What?" Laurel slowed and stared at him through hooded lids. "What did you say?"

"I'm sorry. I can't move. The ropes are too tight."

"Damn. I hadn't thought of that." Laurel twisted to study the various stakes. "But I sure as hell can't untie you. What do I do?"

"There's nothing you can do," Fargo lied.

"Care to bet?" Laurel answered. Giggling at her brainstorm, she eased off of him, reclaimed the toothpick, and knelt beside his left foot. "You don't need to be completely free. Just your legs should be enough." In three strokes she parted the rope, then she swiftly did the same for his right foot. Throwing the knife down, she positioned herself above his organ and winked. "Now let's do this right. And quickly, before the mood is spoiled."

"Whatever you want," Fargo said. He smiled as she fed him into her crack, and when he was all the way in he heaved upward, thrusting his hips as high as he could. Laurel screeched and clung to him.

"Yes! Yes! I want more!"

Fargo gave her what she wanted. In fact, he gave her more than she bargained on, ramming up into her in savage abandon, his strokes so powerful she nearly lost her balance. There was a purpose to his madness, for with each thrust he wrenched at the stakes securing his arms, nearly tearing his arms from their sockets. Repeatedly he arched his back and heaved. He hoped to keep on until he loosened the ropes or the stakes, but he failed to take into account the effect he was having on the redhead.

"I'm coming, big man! I'm coming!"

Fargo could feel her gushing over him. Although he had no intention of doing the same, he could no longer hold back the pent-up urge. He spurted, bucking higher than ever. Laurel trembled and wagged her head, moaning without stop. Her nails raked his chest, his stomach. Without warning she then collapsed, falling onto his chest while her hips continued to pump weakly.

Fargo sank down, exhausted. All his struggling and he had still not loosened either arm. He must try something else or he would be no better off than he had been when he tricked Laurel into making love to him. Craning his neck to the right, he saw that his pants had hitched down around his boots allowing his legs greater freedom. But was it enough?

"You were marvelous," Laurel declared. "I wish I'd met you before I did Rascomb. I'd much rather go back with you."

"It's not too late," Fargo said, giving her this one chance. "Untie me and I'll see that you get to wherever you want to go."

"The offer is tempting," Laurel said, sluggishly sitting up, "but you know I can't accept. If anything went wrong, Rascomb would make a pouch out of my hide, too. No, I'm afraid I have to stick with him."

"Your choice," Fargo said, separating his legs as far as they could go. He waited a few seconds, then scrunched up his face and wriggled his hips.

"What the hell are you doing?" Laurel asked.

"An itch," Fargo said. "I have this bad itch."

"Is that all?" Laurel laughed. "Tell me where it is, lover, and I'll scratch it for you. It's the least I can do after you've been so nice."

"Thank you," Fargo said. He bent his knees outward. "The itch is on the inside of my right leg, close to the knee."

Chuckling, Laurel eased off him and shifted, bending sideways so she could reach the spot. "Here?"

"No. It's lower. Under the knee."

"Here?" Laurel asked, leaning down, which put her head between his thighs.

"A little bit lower," Fargo directed, tensing. She bent even further, and when her neck was level with his upraised legs, he said, "That's it." Laurel applied her nails. He let her scratch for a bit to fool her, to lull her into thinking everything was fine, and then he steeled his sinews, elevated his legs a smidgen higher, and clamped them together with all his might.

"What—?" Laurel blurted, pressing her free hand to his leg.

Fargo squeezed, locking her head in place. She realized she had been duped and tried to jerk loose but he was holding her too tight. Fingernails gouged into him. Her fist flailed at his groin. Fargo swept his knees up toward his chest, unbalancing her, and while she frantically attempted to pull from his grasp, he drove his legs straight down, slamming her face into the ground. There was a thud. Laurel screamed, went into a frenzy. Every ounce of strength he possessed was needed to keep his grip on her neck. He was sure she would succeed in slipping free at any moment, so to forestall her he slammed her face into the ground a second time. And a third.

Laurel Morris sagged, her hands beating ineffectively against Fargo's legs. He maintained the pressure, his thighs as stiff as boards, trying to render her unconscious. His very survival depended on doing so. Laurel's movements became steadily weaker and she wheezed noisily. She tried to speak but only sputtered.

Cramps lanced Fargo's hips and racked his lower back. Ig-

128

noring them, he clamped his legs harder, watching Laurel's arms as they slumped, twitched, and went limp. He held on for another ten seconds for extra measure, then cautiously parted his knees.

Her face beet red, Laurel rolled from between Fargo's legs, onto his belly. Both eyes were closed and she was breathing quietly.

"Finally," Fargo grumbled. Tilting to one side, he rolled her off his body to the ground. He spied the toothpick, lying where she had thrown it close to the right stake. Shifting, he stretched his right leg as far as he could and hooked the knife with the toe of his boot. He was able to pull the toothpick several inches toward him before it fell to one side.

Fargo tried once more, moving slowly and pausing whenever it appeared the knife would slide loose. He was forced to flex his leg outward to drag the toothpick past Laurel. Additional cramps tormented his calf. He had to stop when he had the knife even with his waist because his leg would not bend any further.

Resting a moment, Fargo tried to figure out how he could get his hand on the hilt. The toothpick was a foot and a half from the stake and he had no means of pushing it closer. Or did he? Bracing both arms, he hauled the lower half of his body upward, scraping his backside on some small stones. His shoulders ached terribly and his backbone felt as if it was close to snapping, yet he persisted. Inch by inch he dragged himself higher. Putting the soles of his boots flat, he shoved, the extra boost proving to be all he needed to accomplish the deed.

Fargo inhaled, gathering his energy. There was still very little slack in the ropes, but enough for him to swivel to the right. Making a bridge of his legs over Laurel, Fargo closed his boots on the toothpick, clasping the knife between them. The ropes tore at his wrists as he straightened his legs, working the blade closer and closer. His fingers were numb so he wriggled them to restore the circulation. At last he had the knife near enough; he was able to seize the hilt.

On the verge of freeing himself, Fargo smiled, a smile that changed to a frown when Laurel Morris unexpectedly groaned. He saw her eyelids flutter and realized with dismay that she was coming around much sooner than he had expected.

Quickly he contorted his wrist so he could slash at the rope, but the angle was such that he was unable to bring much pressure to bear.

The redhead groaned louder and her one hand jerked a few times.

Fargo sawed faster, the knife parting strand after strand, but doing so at a snail's pace. Trying not to dwell on what would happen if Laurel revived before he was done, Fargo almost twisted his arm apart cutting furiously.

"What?" Laurel mumbled, and smacked her lips. "Not tonight, Ed. I have a headache."

Pure anguish set Fargo's arm aflame. Bowing his head, he fought an excruciating spasm and methodically pumped his fingers up and down. Strand after strand was severed. Only a few remained when he glanced down and saw Laurel's eyes snap wide. She blinked, apparently confused by her surroundings. Her gaze drifted to his face and the instant they did she voiced a rabid snarl and lunged upward, her nails clawing for his throat. He slapped his legs down, pinning her in place.

"Be patient. I'll get to you in a minute," Fargo said.

"You son of a bitch!" Laurel fumed, thrashing fiercely. There were scrapes and bruises on her face and her left cheek had been split. "I'll kill you for what you've done!"

Teeth sank into Fargo's leg, biting deep, drawing blood. Cursing, he sheared the toothpick through to the stake and pulled. Laurel was opening her mouth to bite again when he touched the blade to her neck. "I wouldn't. Not if you're fond of living."

Simmering hatred gave Laurel the appearance of a hag. "You have the upper hand for now, Trailsman. Enjoy it while it lasts."

"I intend to." Fargo leaned back and sliced into the ropes securing his other wrist. Now that he could move unimpeded, he was free in seconds. Pulling his legs off Laurel, he rose and adjusted his pants. She lay quietly as he located his Colt and checked the cylinder.

"What do you figure on doing with me?"

"Put your clothes on. You'll find out." Fargo saw his hat and shoved it on his head.

"You hoodwinked me, didn't you?" Laurel asked angrily as

she slipped into her underthings. "You were playing me for a fool the whole damn time."

"Not the whole time," Fargo admitted. Surveying the floor area, he spotted a bundle lying among the supplies, a long object wrapped loosely in a ragged blanket. He walked over, unfolded the blanket, and exposed the Sharps. "I thought so," he said.

"Smart man," Laurel baited him.

"I get by," Fargo said, unruffled, which only angered her more.

"You want to know something, Trailsman?" Laurel asked as she plucked her dress from the ground. "I can't wait until Rascomb starts peeling your hide. After what you've done, I think I might even carve a piece or two out of you myself."

"And do you want to know something?" Fargo responded, going up to her. "If you don't keep that mouth of yours closed, I'll stuff it full of whatever is handy to keep you quiet."

Her cheeks coloring red with rage, Laurel put on her dress. She made no further caustic remarks.

"You'll learn yet," Fargo said. Over by the spring stood a sorrel, the only horse left. Nodding at it, he commanded. "Saddle up. We're going for a ride."

Laurel did as instructed. When she was done, Fargo took the reins, touched the barrel of the Sharps to her side, and said, "Now head on up the ravine. And don't try to run off. I won't kill you, but I sure as hell wouldn't mind shooting you in the leg or the foot."

"You bastard," she grumbled.

"What was that?"

"Nothing, smart man."

The Ovaro was where Fargo had tied it. Mounting, he ordered the redhead to climb on the sorrel and together they rode from the brush, up the incline, and out onto the open prairie. A strong westerly lashed the grass, while to the west clouds were forming, the sort of clouds that told Fargo rain would fall by late afternoon. Showers every few days were typical for that time of year, but he was disturbed by the discovery since rain might hamper him if he should have to track down Rascomb or Crane later on.

For about the first hour Laurel Morris held her peace. Then, after glancing at him time and again as if fanning her courage to speak, she asked, "Can I talk?"

"If you spare me the insults."

"I need to know something."

Fargo looked at her.

"I've heard some about you," Laurel said. "You're not the churchgoing kind. You drink, bed doves whenever you're inclined, and you don't back down to any man. You're a lone wolf who does as he damn well pleases, and hang the consequences."

"What's your point?"

"Just this." Laurel pursed her lips. "It doesn't make any sense to me for a man like you to throw in with a bunch of squatters. You're as different from them as night from day. If anything, I should think you'd side with Rascomb." She paused to study his expression. "So why did you? Why'd you take up for them instead of minding your own business and riding on?"

"They needed help."

"That's it? Your only reason?"

"The only one you would understand."

"Come on. Be honest with me. There has to be more to it than that. You're not the Good Samaritan type and don't pretend you are."

Frowning, Fargo rode awhile before he elaborated. "Men and women don't come out of molds. They come out of wombs, and no two are ever alike."

"I never took you for a heavy thinker, either."

The urge to smack her was almost more than Fargo could resist. "We were all children once. There was a time when I was part of a family, with a mother and a father, and we had a nice home of our very own. Not big, or fancy, but nice." He gazed wistfully at the clouds. "Those were happy times. Too bad they didn't last long."

"So deep down, the great Trailsman, the man all hardcases fear, has a heart of gold?" Laurel said, and chortled. "Who would have thought it?"

"I'm not the only one."

"You certainly can't mean me?"

"Who was it that took up with a simple farmer like Ed Morris? Who tried to leave the old life behind and make a whole new start? Who tried as hard as she could to buck her own nature?" Fargo asked. He was shocked when tears filled the redhead's eyes.

"I so wanted us to make our marriage work," she said in a whisper. "I did the best I could until I couldn't take it anymore."

Neither of them uttered a word after that for quite a while. Fargo was slightly in the lead when he saw a tilled field in the distance. "The Walker place. If Rascomb has harmed any of them, I'll show him a few things the Sioux taught me." A thought struck him and he turned. "You mentioned a plan he had. What was it?"

"I don't know if I should tell you. You'll just get all angry—"

"Talk, damn you."

"It involves my daughter."

"Allyson would turn on Samantha? Her best friend?'"

"Rascomb and Crane aren't leaving it up to her to decide. Rascomb got this idea to have Allyson ride up to the Walker place and tell them that she had just gotten away from him. She's to claim that Rascomb has been holding her and me captive and to beg for help to free me."

"What then?" Fargo asked, pushing the stallion faster out of growing fear for Bill's family. They were gullible enough to believe whatever Allyson told them.

"Well, while Allyson keeps them busy telling her story, Rascomb and Crane will sneak up to the house and get the drop on them. Then Rascomb plans to hold the Walkers as hostages. He'll threaten to wipe them out if the other farmers don't load up their wagons and leave."

Simple, but effective. Fargo knew that none of the homesteaders would risk the lives of their friends. They'd do exactly as Rascomb wanted. He rose in the stirrups, trying to catch sight of the sod house, and as he did the wind bore to his ears the blast of gunfire.

13

Fargo pricked his spurs into the Ovaro and shucked his Sharps on the fly. He was too concerned about the Walker family to care what Laurel Morris did, and he assumed she'd dropped behind until the pounding of the sorrel's hoofs proved him wrong. She was striving to keep up with him, but the sorrel was no match for the pinto.

The gunfire was sporadic, There would be a burst of rifle shots, then a brief lull, then more shots.

Fargo recognized the heavy boom of a needle-gun and wished he had ended Crane's lawless career at the Baxter place. Feeding a cartridge into the chamber of his rifle, he yearned to see the tall killer so he could make amends.

Presently the buildings appeared. Guns cracked. Puffs of smoke at the house and at the stable signified where the two sides were holed up. Fargo reined the stallion to the left with the intention of coming up on the stable from the rear. He could only hope that Rascomb and Crane were too preoccupied to spot him before he got there.

The firing from the house rose to a crescendo as the besieged Walkers poured lead into the stable. Fargo suspected that one of them had seen him and they were doing their best to keep Rascomb and Crane pinned down. They did, too, because the answering fire from the stable dried to a trickle.

Twenty yards shy of the southwest corner, Fargo drew rein. Any closer and the two killers might hear the Ovaro. Vaulting to the grass, he ran to the building and crouched next to the wall. Footfalls showed he wasn't alone. Whirling, he glared at Laurel and demanded in a low voice, "What the hell do you think you're doing?"

"My daughter is in there," the redhead replied. "I mean to make sure no harm comes to her."

"Stay put. I'll bring her out."

"Sorry. I can't." Laurel dashed for the rear door.

Fargo grabbed for her arm but missed. "Damn it!" he fumed, rising and trying to overtake her. She would spoil everything by drawing the attention of the gunmen to the back of the stable. He sprinted madly, but Laurel's anxiety over Allyson lent wings to her feet and she reached the door yards ahead of him. Smiling, Laurel laid a hand on the latch.

There was a single shot from within, the roar of the needle-gun, and the door in front of the redhead splintered as the slug tore through it and into her. Laurel was hurled backward, landing on her back in the dust. Struck dumb, she stared blankly over the hole in her chest from which blood was pumping.

Covering the door, Fargo darted to her side and knelt. The bullet had caught her right between the breasts. She had become as pale as a sheet and was opening and closing her mouth like a catfish out of water. Fargo put a hand on her arm and whispered, "Lie still. You'll be better off."

"Oh, God," Laurel croaked. "Not like this. I didn't want it to end like this."

"It was Crane," Fargo said. "They must have spotted us and been waiting for someone to touch the door. They probably figured I'd be the first one through."

"My Allyson?" Laurel said, glancing at the stable. "What if they've hurt her?" She clutched at Fargo and nearly yanked him off balance. "Please. Promise me you'll save her. Swear to me you'll get her to Omaha."

"I'll do what I can."

"Save my precious," Laurel pleaded. She was weakening rapidly and she slumped to the ground at his feet, her arm falling across her wound. "Save her," she repeated, her mouth barely moving.

There was nothing else Fargo could do and he didn't dare stay there, a perfect target for the killers. Whirling, he ran toward the stable and saw the latch moving. He pointed the Sharps, but then held his fire when he realized that it might be Allyson and not Rascomb or Crane. Going prone, he sighted on the crack that appeared as the door slowly opened. The sight of a slender hand and a ruffled sleeve made him glad he had not acted hastily.

Allyson was terrified. She kept glancing back, acting as if she would rather be doing anything than opening that door but was being forced to do so by one of the gunmen. She saw Fargo and went to shout. Then she saw Laurel.

Whatever else might have been said about the mother and daughter, there was no denying they loved one another. The horror and misery that marked Allyson's tortured face were evidence of that. Tears gushed down her cheeks and she took a faltering step.

Inside, a familiar raspy voice snapped, "Do you see him, bitch, or not?"

"My ma!" Allyson bleated forlornly. "Crane shot my ma!"

"I don't care about her. Do you see *him*?"

Fargo had pushed to his feet. As the pair talked, he took two bounds and halted to the left of the doorway, inches from Allyson. She was too addled to notice, even had her vision not been blurred by tears. Holding the Sharps in one hand, he leaned forward, watched her limp fingers slip from the latch, and seized her by the wrist while simultaneously hauling backward. She was fairly catapulted from the doorway. Three shots cracked, pistol shots, the bullets gouging into the door, missing her by a narrow margin.

Bearing Allyson to the ground, Fargo let go and faced the doorway. All was quiet for a while. Allyson lay staring sorrowfully at her mother, her fiery disposition quenched at last.

"Trailsman!" Rascomb called out. "We know you're out there! Why don't you step on in here and we'll settle this man to man?"

Only a rank greenhorn would have fallen for the ruse and answered, and in the process given his position away. Fargo leaned over Allyson and whispered. "Don't move from this spot." He moved to the northwest corner. There was no movement in the house, but he knew the Walker family could see him as he jogged to the northeast corner and stopped. Framed in the window was the grinning face of Jake Larn, who waved and disappeared.

The fool kid, Fargo reflected. On his belly he poked his head out and saw the great door to the stable hanging wide open, as were the hay doors above. Since Rascomb was at the rear of the stable, Fargo guessed that Crane must be close to the front. Just how close might make all the difference in the world.

Fargo crawled around the corner, his skin prickling. He was too vulnerable for his liking, but this was the only way to settle accounts with the two killers. Burning them out, which would destroy Walker's stable, couldn't be done. Waiting them out would take far too long, and before they went down Rascomb or Crane might take a few more innocents with them. Fargo was determined to end it right then.

Fifteen feet from the entrance, Fargo slowed. He counted on hearing a cough or rustling as the pair moved around so he could pin down where they were. Unfortunately, silence reigned. Fargo crawled to within a yard of the door and halted. Seconds went by, adding up to a full minute. He thought of Allyson, helpless and unprotected, and knew he couldn't wait forever. Removing his hat, he edged nearer to the opening.

The scrape of metal on wood brought Fargo's gaze to the hay doors where a rifle barrel was sliding outward. The shape verified it was the needle-gun, slanting at the house.

Fargo tilted outward, trying to see Crane. The tall killer was too well-screened by the right-hand hay door for Fargo to get a glimpse of him, let alone a clear shot. He wondered if Larn or Walker had noticed the needle-gun, and had an upsetting thought: What if Crane was taking a bead on someone? What if it was Samantha or Maggy?

The fear brought instant action. Fargo tucked the Sharps to his shoulder, calculated the approximate spot where Crane must be crouched, and fired through the hay door. A high-pitched yelp like that of a stricken coyote testified to his accuracy. The needle-gun fell out of the loft and to the ground.

"I'm hit, Rascomb!" Crane cried. "I'm hit!"

Fargo made a split-second choice. Should he reload and lie there hoping for another shot or should he carry the fight to the hardcases while they were flustered? Setting the Sharps down, he drew his Colt, brought his knees up, and hurtled inside. The center aisle was empty, the rear door still open. Fargo cut to the right so his back would be to the wall, and he saw the ladder to the hayloft move. He froze when a boot hooked on a rung. Then the other foot materialized.

"Rascomb? Where are you?"

Crane descended quickly, grunting each time he lowered a leg. His right shoulder was bloody, his shirt sporting a hole. He was gazing toward the back of the stable and consequently didn't see Fargo until only one rung from the bottom. "You!" he bellowed, his lips curving over his teeth.

"Me," Fargo responded. "Don't move and you might live."

"Go to hell!" Crane roared, hopping to the floor and clawing at his six-gun. The revolver was on his right hip, and with his right arm unusable he had to draw with his left, an awkward feat under ideal circumstances. Wounded as he was, and with the pistol butt angled behind him, he performed the cross draw with fumbling fingers and paid the price for his stupidity.

Fargo worked the trigger twice, shooting from the hip, his elbow slightly bent. Each shot drove the tall killer backward. Crane smacked into a stall, doubled at the waist, and pitched onto his face. Fargo ducked low, expecting Rascomb to respond in kind, but there were no answering shots, no sounds whatsoever from anywhere in the stable. He moved to the right, to the first stall, directly across from where Crane was sprawled.

"Trailsman? Can you hear me?"

Wary of a trap, Fargo didn't answer. The shout came from outside, from out back, and suddenly a shadow filled the doorway. He extended the Colt but eased up on the trigger when he saw the gunman's helpless shield.

"I'll shoot her if you don't show yourself," Rascomb threatened, giving Allyson a shove with his shoulder. He had an arm locked on her throat and his revolver pressed to her head. "She means nothing to me," he declared. "So don't think I won't do as I say."

To step into the open was a death warrant. Fargo scanned the stable, seeking a means of taking Rascomb by surprise. There were none.

"I won't wait forever," Rascomb warned, stopping Allyson a dozen feet inside. "I'll count to three, If you haven't shown by then, you can bury this bitch next to her mother." Pausing, he licked his lips. "One."

Fargo reached into his boot, extracted the Arkansas tooth-pick, raised it behind his neck, and swiftly slipped the slender blade under the collar of his buckskin shirt. He adjusted his neckerchief so that the knot held the hilt against his neck.

"Two!" Rascomb shouted.

Letting the Colt droop so it hung upside down from his trig-ger finger, Fargo double-checked the toothpick. He couldn't afford a single mistake.

"Three!"

"Here I am!" Fargo cried, rising with his arms out from his sides. "Don't kill her."

Rascomb swung behind Allyson, a single beady eye peering past her shoulder. "Step into the open so I can see you," he in-structed. "And lose the hardware."

Fargo dropped the Colt into the hay as he strode to the mid-dle of the aisle. Without being ordered, he elevated his arms so his hands were close to his ears. "Let her go," he said. "This is just between the two of us."

Rascomb, his confidence bolstered by seeing Fargo un-armed, straightened and took a half step to the right, exposing half of his body. "I didn't figure you'd really do it," he said. "What's this woman to you?"

"Nothing. Nothing at all."

"Yet you're going to die because of her?" Rascomb slapped Allyson on the back of the head, causing her to cringe. "She's not worth it, Fargo. She's just an uppity snot who thinks the sun rises and sets between her legs."

"Let her go," Fargo persisted. He needed Allyson out of the way so he could throw the toothpick without the risk of strik-ing her by accident.

"Maybe I want to keep her," Rascomb said, entwining his fingers in her luxuriant hair and twisting. "Maybe I want some company on that long trail to Omaha."

"You'll never get there."

"Who is going to stop me? You?" Rascomb laughed and jabbed his six-shooter in the air. "You're dead and you don't even know it yet."

"I should have expected as much," Fargo said, changing his tactics. "Only a coward would hide behind a woman's skirts.

And I've known all along that you have a yellow streak down your spine a mile wide."

Rascomb, bristling, shoved Allyson to the left, into an empty stall. "Now who's a coward?" he growled. He advanced several paces, glowering savagely, and aimed at Fargo's chest. "I've rubbed out a lot of people in my time, Trailsman, but I've never wanted to kill anyone as much as I do you."

Fargo's right hand was resting on the side of his neck, an inch from the throwing knife. He couldn't expect to beat a bullet, but if he could throw the toothpick at the same time Rascomb fired he'd die having the satisfaction of taking Rascomb with him. His palm covered the hilt, his fingers curled.

Allyson Morris abruptly uttered a piercing wail, placed her hands over her eyes, and started crying hysterically. She leaned against the stall, her whole body shaking.

At her outburst, Rascomb glanced around in annoyance. "Shut the hell up!" he barked. He looked back at Fargo, then at her again as she blubbered louder. "Didn't you hear me, damn it? I can't hear myself think."

Fargo was ready. He didn't take his eyes off Rascomb, and when the grimy killer glanced again at Allyson, he streaked his arm up and around. His entire frame whipped into the throw, every sinew a taut wire. Because Rascomb wore a black wool coat, and the blade might not go all the way through it, Fargo threw high rather than low. The toothpick's steel sparkled in the light from the rear door.

Rascomb must have seen the knife out of the corner of his eye. He tried to skip to one side but was a shade too slow. The toothpick caught him on the throat, burning into him like a red-hot brand. He screamed as he tottered backward. Automatically he grabbed the knife and tugged it loose, which transformed his throat into a spurting mess. Whining pathetically, he looked up and lifted his Colt.

Fargo was caught dead to rights. He lunged to the left, knowing Rascomb would nail him, and actually flinched when the stable rocked to two gun blasts. The sight of Rascomb crumpling puzzled him until he belatedly realized the shots had come from the front of the stable, not the rear.

"So that's what you keep in your boot? Handy little neck-blister, ain't it? I reckon I'll have to get me one of them sometime."

Turning, Fargo gave Jake Larn a grateful smile. "This is twice now you've saved me. I hope I can return the favor one day."

Larn had on his pants and his unbuttoned white shirt, and nothing else. New bandages covered his chest. His bare feet kicked up puffs of dirt as he entered, chuckling. "The sad part is that no one will ever believe me if I go around bragging that I saved the Trailsman's life. Everyone will brand me an out-and-out liar."

Shadows danced in the entrance as the Walkers filled the great door. Bill had his rifle. Maggy clutched a pistol. Samantha went to Larn and put a hand on his arm. "Are you all right?" she asked.

"Never better," the cocky gunman answered, and winked at her. "But I'm beginning to wonder how our friend Fargo has lasted so long. He has a knack for getting into tight spots."

Strident sobbing wafted to the rafters as Allyson shuffled into the aisle and headed for the back door. She moved mechanically, her limbs wooden, tears streaming down her face.

"Ally!" Samantha called, rushing to her friend's aid. Maggy also went to the heartbroken woman, and together they turned her around and steered Allyson out the front.

Fargo collected his Colt and was wiping the toothpick off on Rascomb's pants when Bill Walker said his name.

"This one is still alive."

Crane had been rolled over and propped against the stall. His eyes were open, but dim, and from his heavy breathing it was clear he would not last long. He looked at Fargo as Fargo squatted. "You think you've won, but you haven't."

"Rascomb is dead. You're the last one. It's over."

A strangled laugh gurgled from Crane's throat. "I'm not the last one, bastard. There's one you've missed."

"Can that be true?" Bill Walker asked uneasily. "Are we never to know a moment's peace?"

Larn shook his head. "Don't pay no attention to this peckerwood. He's done for, so he's trying to get back at us the only way he can. It's just words."

"You keep thinking that, idiot," Crane said.

"I'd know if there was someone else," Larn responded. "I was with the gang from the very first."

"But you weren't told all there was to know," Crane struggled. Pain made him bow his head and wheeze for a bit. Then he glanced at them, grinning viciously. "You don't even know who the boss is, you dumb kid." His hands shook as he attempted to raise them and failed. "There's a lot you weren't told, Larn. And it was the same with the rest. The only one Rascomb trusted completely was me."

"You're blowing hot air," Larn insisted.

Fargo slipped the toothpick into his ankle sheath, arranged his pant leg properly, and rose. "No, he's not," he said somberly. "There's one we've overlooked."

Some of Crane's arrogance evaporated. "Got it all figured out, do you?"

"I've known since Nightmare killed Baxter's stock."

"Like hell. There were no tracks to give it away."

"That was why I became suspicious," Fargo said. "That, and the fact mountain lions can't work latches."

"Doesn't matter," Crane blustered. "You don't stand a prayer. He'll be ready for you."

"Who will?" Bill Walker asked. "Who are you talking about?"

"Why should I tell you, you rotten nester?" Crane replied. He sneered in contempt, stiffened, and abruptly died, the sneer indelibly lining his bitter features.

"He's no great loss," Larn said, giving Crane a shove with his foot that knocked the tall killer to the ground. "I never met such a hateful man in all my born days."

"We might as well bury them now and get it over with," Fargo proposed.

Bill Walker produced a pair of spades and led Fargo to a point forty yards from the stable where a patch of weeds grew. For the next hour they toiled at digging three graves. The bodies of Rascomb and Crane were carted out and laid to rest without ceremony, their graves left unmarked.

With Laurel Morris it was different. A crude wooden cross was driven into the upturned earth. Walker had his wife and daughter escort Allyson to the site, and then he read excerpts from the good book while everyone else bowed their heads and Allyson cried softly.

The Ovaro was grazing with two of Walker's horses. Fargo road the pinto to the corral, tied it at the water trough, and went into the house. Maggy prepared a modest meal, but the only one with any appetite was Jake Larn. As he stuffed biscuits into his mouth, the young gunman watched Fargo checking the Sharps and the Colt. "Want me to come along?" he asked.

"I'll handle this alone."

"Two guns are always better than one."

"I'm the one he jumped from behind. I'm the one who owes him."

The Walkers were all listening. "It's Gar you're going after, isn't it?" Maggy inquired.

"Yes, ma'am," Fargo confirmed.

"Was he in cahoots with Rascomb all along?" Bill asked.

"It appears that way. Whoever hired Rascomb was taking no chances. When he saw that Rascomb was having a hard time driving you off, he must have hired Gar as added insurance." Fargo faced them. "Think back. Did Nightmare's attacks begin before or after Gar showed up?"

Bill Walker scratched his chin. "Now that you mention it, that cougar didn't give us any trouble until after Gar showed on the scene. We'd seen tracks, of course, and once or twice we'd spotted the lion, but it didn't bother our stock at all at first."

"But how did Gar pull it off?" Samantha asked. "Tom Baxter swore he saw a mountain lion that night."

"He thought he did," Fargo said. "If I'm right, I'll be able to show you how Gar did it after I get back." Standing, he walked to the door, then paused. "Jake, you look after these people while I'm gone."

"You've no need to worry," Larn said. "I was the one who saved their bacon this morning when I wouldn't let them go running off with Allyson. I knew not to trust her." He chuckled. "Must have made Rascomb as mad as a wet hen. Crane and him were hiding in the stable, and when they saw we weren't coming out, they snapped off a few shots."

"Jake saved us," Samantha said tenderly.

"If Gar gets past me, he might have to do it again," Fargo said. "All of you should stay inside for a while. It'll be safer." Touching his hat brim, he stepped out into the bright sunlight, climbed on the stallion, and made straight for the Platte River.

14

The cottonwoods and willows were being whipped to a frenzy by the intensifying wind when Skye Fargo reached the south bank and turned westward. His Sharps rested across his thighs and his Colt rested loosely in his holster. He had no illusions about what would happen if Gar spotted him before he spotted Gar, so he rode with extra vigilance.

Some men were more dangerous than others. A skilled gunman more so than a farmer. A soldier more so than a storekeeper. An Apache more so than a Hopi. A seasoned hunter and trapper like Gar was one of the most dangerous of all, a man who could move like a ghost, blend into vegetation as if invisible, and who might strike from any direction at any time.

So Fargo's nerves were on edge as he slowly neared the location of the dugout. He entertained the hope he would catch the giant unawares, but knew better. Gar's senses were more like those of an animal than a human. Worse, Gar would be on the lookout for him after their fight at the farm.

The same wall of undergrowth as before barred Fargo's path. Cradling the Sharps in his elbow, Fargo swung down and entered the maze on foot. On horseback he not only made more noise, he would be easier to pick off. The woodland was quiet as he worked along the winding trail. No squirrels chattered. No birds sang. This was a bad sign, since wildlife only hushed up when predators or humans were abroad. Or, as in this case, a human predator.

Fargo slowed at every turn and switchback to survey the next stretch. At times he had the sensation unseen eyes were on him, but he never saw anyone. He was mildly surprised that he made it through the maze unchallenged. Once in the open he crouched behind a bush.

The giant's horse was gone. The dugout appeared deserted. No smoke curled from the ventilation hole and the door hung wide open.

Highly suspicious, Fargo moved closer to the trapper's lair. He saw several hides hanging from the ropes and a pile of beaver traps next to a tree stump. The whistling wind smothered all sounds, even his own footsteps.

At the door Fargo hesitated to peer into the gloomy confines. Smaller traps lay near the opening. Farther back strips of dried meat hung on pegs that had been driven into the earth walls. Several unfinished pelts lay scattered about. Fargo inched into the dugout but repeatedly glanced outside. A reeking stench churned his stomach, and he spied the heaped entrails of skinned animals in one corner. A rumpled blanket spread out in another corner was Gar's bedding. A few supplies were stacked next it.

The Spartan accommodations held scant interest for Fargo. He pivoted on a heel and was leaving when a bulky bundle partly hidden in the shadows caught his eyes. Going over, he examined his find, nodded, and carried the bundle out.

It was another hide, only unlike any of the others. Great care had been taken in curing it so that the pelt was as soft as goose down, the hair all intact. Fargo leaned the Sharps against a tree and unrolled the hide to its full length of nearly seven feet from the peaked ears to the tip of the tail, which had been left on along with the legs.

"Find what you wanted, puny man?"

At the gruff shout, Fargo whirled and grabbed the Sharps. He scanned the undergrowth but saw no sign of the trapper. "Why don't you step on out here, Gar, where I can see you?"

"And spoil Gar's fun? Not yet."

By the sound of the voice Fargo could tell the giant was moving. He nudged the hide with a toe and called out. "Did you have much trouble killing the male cougar?"

"Not at all. Gar strung up a deer and when the cat came to eat, Gar shot him."

"Was it your idea to cover yourself with the hide and slaughter the farmers' stock?" Fargo asked, trying to keep the trapper talking so he could pin down where Gar was. But the wily giant had reversed direction and seemed further away when next he spoke.

"Gar is pretty clever. Not as stupid as everyone likes to believe." A pause ensued. "You knew, didn't you?"

"Yes."

"How?"

"There were no tracks at the Baxters', just smudge marks. What did you do? Wrap beaver hides around your feet?"

"You're smart, too, puny man." Now the voice came from somewhere else. "But you don't know it all."

"Did the man who hired you offer you a lot of money?" Fargo asked. He then moved swiftly to the right and took cover beside the dugout.

For a minute no answer was forthcoming. "Gar will earn three hundred dollars for his part in driving the squatters off. Three hundred more than the one hundred Gar was already paid." This time the yell came from the brush to the south.

"What's his name, Gar? Who wants the farmers to leave?"

"That is Gar's secret."

"Some friend you turned out to be. The farmers treated you like one of their own and you betray them," Fargo said to anger the giant. "Is that any way to thank them for letting you come to their socials?"

There was no reply.

Fargo glanced at the cougar pelt. "Tell me something, Gar. How did you make the claw marks look so real? I saw the butchered stock and I almost couldn't tell the difference between those a real lion would make and those you did."

Rumbling laughter came from the southeast. "Gar will soon show you, puny man. And it will be the last thing you ever see."

Fargo thought he spied a hulking shape deep in the brush but he couldn't be certain. "You haven't killed any of the farmers, Gar, so I'll give you this one chance. Ride on out and I'll let you live."

"You have it backwards. Gar is staying. And so are you, three feet under."

Fleeting movement was the only clue Fargo had to the giant's position. He raised the Sharps but there was no one to shoot. Stymied, he tried to move around the back of the dugout, but the river was lapping at the bottom of the north wall and he didn't care to get his boots wet. They might squish when he walked, enabling Gar to easily locate him.

Moving close to the door, Fargo scanned the tangled vegetation. He had two basic choices; either he went after the giant or he waited for the giant to come after him. He was fairly safe where he was—Gar couldn't get near him without being spotted—but it went against Fargo's grain to wait around to be attacked. And since he had learned the art of stalking from masters of the craft, namely Sioux warriors, he felt confident enough to venture from the dugout into the undergrowth south of it.

First Fargo tried to spot the giant's legs by crouching low. He saw countless limbs and twigs and clumps of grass and weeds, but not any legs. Next Fargo tried standing on a boulder and peering over the top of the brush. He saw a sea of branches broken by intermittent clearings, but not the head and shoulders of the titan hunting him.

Going to ground under a thicket, Fargo elected to wait for some sound to give the trapper away. He waited, and waited, and he might as well have had wax plugs in his ears for all the sounds he heard. He'd expected Gar to be a formidable enemy. Only now did he appreciate just *how* formidable.

Fargo sneaked to the edge of the brush to check the clearing and the dugout. Both were undisturbed, as he'd left them. He was turning back into the vegetation when he looked at the dugout door and discovered that it was shut. And he clearly recalled it being wide open before.

Grinning at how brainlessly the giant had trapped himself, Fargo glided up to the dugout and crouched. The Sharps was already cocked and set. With a finger on the trigger, he gripped the door with his other hand and yanked it open while at the same time he snapped, "Got you!"

But no one was there. The dugout was empty. Fargo blinked, perplexed, and slowly rose. He figured the wind had blown the door closed and he faced toward the brush, and the moment he did loud splashing erupted to his rear. Fargo tried to spin, to level the rifle. He had hardly begun when massive arms encircled him and he was jerked bodily into the air and shaken much like helpless prey in the grip of a powerful grizzly. His top and bottom teeth cracked together. The rifle barrel smacked against his shin.

"Now, puny man, Gar has his fun."

Fargo felt the giant shift toward the dugout, felt the giant take long, rapid, strides. With a start he realized what the trapper was about to do and he brought his legs up to absorb some of the shock as he was propelled into the door face first. Stars exploded before his eyes. Wood shattered. Torment seared his ankles. The blow dazed him, leaving him slumped in the giant's arms.

"Don't go to sleep on Gar," Gar said and laughed uproariously. "I want you to last awhile."

Fargo was flung to the earth. The Sharps was ripped from his hand and the Colt lifted free. Iron fingers gouged into his shoulders and he was raised on high and shaken again. The shaking cleared his vision.

"So you came to stop Gar?" the giant said, smirking. "But it's Gar who will stop you. And when Gar is done, he will go see Samantha Walker and ask her to dance."

"She doesn't dance with jackasses," Fargo mumbled, counting on the affront to so outrage the giant that Gar would hurl him to the ground, thus giving him a chance to get to the toothpick. He was lifted even higher and he braced for the impact.

"You like to insult Gar. Let's see if you can insult Gar under water."

A rush of air fanned Fargo's back and his hat flew off as he sailed into the Platte River. He got his mouth closed but was unable to take much of a breath. The clammy water closed around him; everything was a blur. His knees hit bottom. Bending his head back, he pushed off, angling for the surface. Suddenly a bulky form blocked out the light and huge hands seized him by the front of his shirt. He was shoved deeper. Water was in his nose, his ears. He punched the arms but it was similar to punching solid wood. His blows had no effect.

Fargo's lungs ached abominably. His head swam, and he had difficulty telling which way was up and which was down. He tried kicking the trapper but missed. Weakness overcame him and he seemed to be floating in ink.

"Not yet!"

The words hardly registered, but fresh air and sunshine did. Fargo came to life, gasping for breath. The trees seemed to bob as Gar tramped ashore.

"Can you bounce, little man?"

Bounce? Fargo wondered, and as the full meaning hit him, he hit the ground with bone-wrenching force, causing his left elbow to go completely numb. He wanted to leap up, to pound Gar to a pulp, but his body wouldn't cooperate. Never had he been so helpless against another man and it put a bitter taste in his mouth.

"Are you tired so soon?"

Fargo was grasped by the back of the collar, hoisted to his knees, and thrown at a tree. Somehow he twisted and missed the trunk. Landing on his shoulders, he rolled, then lay still, his knees tucked to his chest. He only had one hope. He must flee into the brush and hide, buy time to recover. Otherwise his days of wandering were over.

Gripping the Arkansas toothpick, Fargo listened to the lumbering tread of the giant as it grew louder and louder. A hand fell on his shoulder. Fargo lashed around, spearing the blade into the giant's upper thigh, slicing as he did. Gar roared and swung without thinking.

Fargo was cuffed on the side of the head and sent tumbling. He came out of the tumble in a lurching run for the undergrowth. The giant was still roaring and doubled over, an enormous palm covering the bloody wound.

"Gar will kill you now, puny man!"

Not, Fargo reflected, if he had a say in the matter. Barreling into the brush, he darted to the right, traveled a dozen feet, and darted to the left, staying low the whole time. His legs wobbled, but he forged on, swatting branches aside, until he could go no further. Totally exhausted, he slumped to the ground and crawled under a thicket. Here, at last, he felt safe.

It sounded as if a bull buffalo was loose in the maze. Undergrowth crackled and snapped or was crunched underfoot. A furious Gar was plowing mindlessly to the right and left, uprooting whole bushes in his wrath. "Where are you?" he bellowed. "Where the hell are you?"

Fargo tensed when the crackling drew closer, then relaxed when the giant moved in the other direction. He rubbed his elbow, trying to restore feeling. Without his guns, the odds were against him, but he decided not to make a run for them. Gar might be anticipating just such a move.

Suddenly the racket ceased. Fargo rose on his good elbow and peered out through a crack in the thicket. Gar had vanished and must be lying low waiting for him to make a mistake. The hunter had become the hunted.

Lying down, Fargo took stock. He still had the toothpick, and the Ovaro wasn't all that far away. A short ride to the Walker place and he could return with another pistol and rifle and this time finish Gar off. But he didn't like the idea of running off. He didn't think Gar had a gun, so they were evenly matched, or as evenly matched as they could be given the giant's tremendous size.

Fargo looked around again. He felt strong enough to crawl out and crouch. Then, taking slow step after slow step, he painstakingly worked his way southward, further from the Platte. He had to pick his way through the brush at times and once, when he snapped a twig underfoot, he remained motionless for over five minutes, until satisfied Gar had not heard. Eventually he slipped from the dense growth forming the maze and was in more open woodland.

Sliding from tree to tree, Fargo moved along the perimeter until he saw a willow with a fork low to the ground. Into this he climbed. Shielded by the drooping boughs, he went up over eight feet and stopped to rest and search. Such a vantage point should have given him a clear view of the trapper, yet it didn't. He could see a portion of the dugout, and the Ovaro, but not hide nor hair of Gar.

Staying there awhile brought no results, either. Fargo slipped to the ground and covered a short distance when he saw five or six downed saplings off to the right. Some force of nature had felled them months ago; the wood was dead but stout. He selected the thinnest, which was no thicker than his wrist. Concealing himself again, he crouched and stripped off all the slender, brittle branches. Then he whittled the thick end into a tapered point. The end result was a makeshift spear.

Fargo hefted it, testing the balance. He tucked the blade of the toothpick under his belt, grasped the spear in both hands, and resumed stalking the giant. Soon he was near the spot where he had left the stallion. Creeping along, he suddenly spied an enormous shape on the ground twenty yards in front of him.

Gar was on his stomach in a patch of high grass, a long knife glinting in his right hand. He was watching the pinto, and evidently had been for quite a while.

Fargo held the spear at chest height and furtively advanced. Always on the lookout for twigs or dry grass, he only moved each foot a few inches with every step. Whenever Gar moved, Fargo froze. Judging by the number of times Gar fidgeted, the giant was becoming impatient and might not stay there much longer. A single cottonwood was all that separated Fargo from the trapper when Gar unexpectedly rose to his knees and looked suspiciously around.

Partially screened by the tree trunk, Fargo halted. He needed to be closer for an effective thrust. But Gar was showing no inclination to lie back down. Rather, the giant sensed something was wrong and was probing the maze and the bank of the river.

A flurry of wings out on the Platte heralded the arrival of a small flock of ducks. They alighted gracefully on the surface and swam upriver.

Gar appeared satisfied all was well. Silently he flattened, his knife hand next to his right shoulder.

Fargo, the spear angled downward, continued around the cottonwood. Four steps were all he had to take. The first two went well. But on the third step his sole brushed the tops of the grass as he set his foot down. The sound he made was so slight that only the keenest of ears could have heard.

And the giant did. He twisted and started to rise.

Springing forward, Fargo lanced the tip at Gar's chest. Gar flung himself to one side and was spared a fatal stab, but the spear tore through his shirt and raked his ribs, drawing blood. Slashing with the knife, Gar tried to sever Fargo's throat. An upward sweep of the spear blocked the blow and Fargo, trying to close in, was held at bay when Gar swung the blade at his legs. Fargo had to back-pedal, which gave the trapper space to rise.

"Always the tricky one," Gar said.

"It ends here," Fargo responded, the spear now at his waist to counter the knife.

"Gar thinks so, too," the giant declared. He was calm, even grinning, as confident of his prowess as ever. "You should have run away when you had the chance."

Fargo was watching the trapper's eyes. In a fight, a man's eyes often gave away his strategy before his body moved to carry it out, and this instance was no different. He saw the corners narrow and knew Gar was going to do something. The giant fell into a low crouch, swiped once more at Fargo's legs, and, when Fargo lowered the spear to parry, Gar snapped upright and chopped at Fargo's head.

The narrow end of the branch saved Fargo's life. He was swinging the sharp end up to defend himself and the narrow end deflected the blade. Strictly unintentional, but it impressed Gar. The giant scowled and circled, seeking another opening, feinting and stabbing as the whim hit him.

Fargo flicked the spear in response, never letting the knife score. He had to keep backing up to prevent Gar from getting too close. After a minute of this cat-and-mouse he realized the giant was doing it on purpose, and was herding him in a specific direction—toward the river.

Fargo attempted to move to the right, but Gar skipped in front of him. He tried going left with the same result. A backward look showed him the bank loomed behind him, a steep section four feet high. Fargo came to the brink and halted.

"Gar will tell you something, puny man," the trapper said. "No one has ever lasted this long against Gar. You are the best Gar has ever fought."

"You must not have fought very many men," Fargo commented, thinking if he could make Gar mad, Gar might become reckless. "I'll bet women and children are more to your liking."

The ploy worked, all too well. Predictably, Gar was incensed, and he let his anger get the better of his judgment. Roaring, he sprang, heedless of the spear tip Fargo streaked at his neck. He batted it aside without much effort, coiled his legs, and jumped.

Fargo had nowhere to go. He was swept over the edge and into the Platte, only this time he squirmed loose as they splashed down and was on his feet before Gar. He also contrived to hold on to the spear, which he drove at the giant's midsection.

Gar's ponderous hand closed on the tip, and with a surge of his rippling muscles he yanked the spear out of Fargo's grasp and pitched it to the shore. "What will you do now?" he gloated.

In answer, Fargo drew the toothpick. The slender blade seemed so puny compared to the immense trapper, but it was all he had. He retreated downriver along the high bank, looking for a low point where he could clamber out.

"No, you don't," Gar said, following and jabbing playfully with his knife. None of the strokes had his full strength behind them. He was toying with Fargo, taking his sweet time.

Fargo went faster, but the giant kept pace. He saw where the slope wasn't as steep and made a bid to scramble up it. Gar lunged, and when Fargo ducked he lost his footing and slipped back into the river, but only to his waist.

"Clumsy," the giant mocked him.

Turning, Fargo ran, determined to get far enough ahead of the trapper that he could climb out without interference. The water swirled around his legs, slowing him slightly. He pumped harder, casting looks over his shoulder. Gar was running but was not in any hurry. Maybe, Fargo reasoned, Gar wanted to tire him.

Fargo had gone ten feet when a stake appeared. He saw the chain, partially camouflaged with dirt and leaves, winding down into the water, and distinguished the outline of the beaver trap at the base of the bank. He also remembered the grisly fate that once befell a mountain man who had been careless when setting a trap out. His lips a grim line, Fargo ran until he was almost abreast of the trap, then he pretended to trip over his own feet and fell onto his knees. He even cried out as if in pain. Doubled over, he fumbled under the water for the heavy springs, actually curved metal pieces, that protruded on either side of the trap. Starting to lift, he glanced back at Gar, who was smiling and stabbing the big knife at his back. And then, his body a blur, Fargo swung the trap completely around, directly into the path of Gar's arm.

Gar was unable to check the swing. Astonishment claimed

154

him an instant before his knife struck the trigger pan and the jagged steel jaws closed with a sharp snap onto his wrist. The heavy jaws sheared clean through the flesh and deep into the bone, so deep the wrist was nearly severed. Blood spurted wildly.

Fargo barreled into the giant, the dripping toothpick in his right hand. Once, twice, three times he sank the blade into Gar's chest above the heart. Gar tottered and gawked dumbly at him in disbelief at the rapid turnabout.

"Gar can't—," the giant said. A convulsion silenced him. His eyes rolled upward, his legs shook, and, his mouth agape, he crashed onto his back. Then he was still, his mighty frame slowly sinking.

Skye Fargo wiped a hand across his brow as the water flowing past his legs changed from a muddy brown to a dark shade of red.

15

A weary and battered Skye Fargo stared at the rippling ranks of grass before him as he rode slowly toward the Walker farm, while to the west a thunderstorm swept over the pristine prairie. Muted rumbling and crackling, like the booming of distant cannon, testified to the severity of the storm.

Tied in a roll behind the cantle was the male cougar skin along with another item Fargo had found when he gave the dugout a thorough search after he had slain Gar. It resembled a wooden war club, except that five nails had been pounded through the knobby head, each about half an inch apart, and the nails had been bent downward so that they mimicked the hooked claws of a mountain lion. This was how Gar had fooled the farmers into thinking a mountain lion was responsible for slaying their stock.

Fargo had found one other thing: a poke containing the money Gar had been paid in advance for his services, money Fargo was going to give to the farmers to divide up among them as they saw fit. After the nightmare they had suffered, they were entitled.

The sod house came into sight and Fargo goaded the pinto to go a bit faster. After so many days of little rest, of constantly being on the move, of one fight for his life after another, he longed for nothing more than ten hours or so of uninterrupted sleep. Then he would bid the farmers good-bye and resume his journey westward.

Fargo was approaching the house from the northwest, from the rear, and so he had no idea that the Walkers had visitors until he angled more toward the front corner and spied four horses tied at the corral. A few more steps of the pinto and he saw the four newcomers.

They were four men, three with tied down holsters and another in an expensive suit and bowler hat, fanned out in a line and facing the house. The three gunmen wore hard expressions typical of their breed. Not a man was smiling.

Fargo's intuition blared and he quickly turned the stallion before the four could spot him and headed for the rear corner instead. He didn't know what was going on but he didn't much like the way it appeared and he was taking no chances. The far-off thunder helped to disguise the clumping of the pinto's heavy hoofs, so he was able to reach the sod house undetected.

Alighting on the balls of his feet, Fargo inched to the front corner, pressed an ear to the edge, and listened. The first words he heard were those spoken by Bill Walker.

"—care who you are, I want you off my property and I want you off now. And take your gun-sharks with you."

Someone sighed. "For the life of me I don't comprehend why you farmers are being so stubborn about this. Legally, the land isn't even yours, yet you refuse to listen to reason and do the right thing."

"I know I speak for all of us, Mr. Becker, when I say that we have too much invested here to leave. This is prime farm land, and one day there will be thousands of homesteaders here just like us. You wait and see. The Nebraska Territory will be the breadbasket of the whole country."

Fargo took off his hat and slid an eye to the corner. Becker, the man in the finely tailored suit, was not a happy man.

"Frankly, Mr. Walker, I don't give a damn about farmers or farming. All that concerns me is that I need this strip of land you and the others have settled on and I refuse to take no for an answer."

Bill Walker stood closest to the four men. Behind him, from right to left, were Maggy, Samantha, and Jake Larn. Only the young gunman and Bill were armed, but Walker carelessly held his rifle in the crook of an arm, pointed at the ground, and would be unable to bring it into play before one of the three hardcases put several slugs into him. As Fargo watched, Larn took a step forward and snorted.

"I should say you don't take no for an answer, mister! That's why you hired Rascomb, and I reckon Gar, too, to drive these fine folks off. Too bad you wasted your money."

"Rascomb was a great disappointment," Becker conceded. "I'm not the least bit sorry to hear he's dead." He smiled, the smile of a snake coated in slime. "But that's all water under the bridge, as the saying goes. I became impatient with the state of affairs and decided to come here personally to persuade all of you to leave. And to prove my sincerity, I'm prepared to offer each and every farmer the sum of eight hundred dollars for his place."

Bill Walker whistled, and Fargo didn't blame him. Eight hundred dollars was a lot of money to men who seldom saw more than a hundred and fifty dollars at one time in their entire lives. He wondered if Walker would be tempted.

"That's a very generous offer," the farmer declared, "but my answer is still no. You see, this is our *home* now. I know it doesn't mean much to a man like you, but to us it's everything."

"You're a fool, Walker," Becker said.

"He sure is," Jake Larn said sarcastically. "I can't imagine him not wanting to make a deal with the son of a bitch who drove off some of his friends and beat others, then tried to have him killed. It just ain't logical."

Becker glared at the grinning gunman. "Just who the hell are you, anyway?"

"I'm hurt that you don't know me," Larn said. "Didn't Rascomb tell you about the men he hired?"

"You're on *my* payroll?" Becker asked in amazement.

"I was, then the stink of those other polecats started to rub off on me and I came to my senses."

One of the hired guns with Becker, a lanky man in a black hat, glanced at his boss and said, "I know this kid, Mr. Becker. He goes around shooting off his mouth as much as he does his pistol. I can take him if you want. Just say the word."

Jake Larn laughed. "You couldn't take me if both my hands were tied behind my back, Schultz."

Bill Walker held up a hand. "I won't have any violence! There has been far too much already! If you men won't be civil, you'll have to leave."

Becker raised his bowler to rub a hand through his sparse hair. "You just don't see it, do you, dirt farmer?" he snapped as he adjusted the hat in place. "I'm going to have your property whether you agree to sell or not. The same goes for every last one of you. I have too much at stake, too much invested, to do otherwise."

"What, exactly, do you have at stake, sir?" Walker inquired. "If I might ask," he added politely.

The man in the bowler gave each of the three gunmen a meaningful look, then casually slid a hand under his jacket. "It doesn't matter now whether you learn the truth or not, so I'll tell you." He gestured eastward. "In a year or so the government will be opening the territory to settlement, and when that happens I aim to lay a claim to a strip of land along the Platte from Omaha clear to Fort Laramie."

The idea struck Bill Walker as so preposterous that he cackled. "Tarnation. The government will never let one man claim so much."

"If the man has a lot of political influence, and if the man has agreed to pay pittances to a number of others who will file original claims and then sell to him, that man can buy as much land as he wants," Becker said.

"But whatever for? Why would you want all that acreage?"

"I can answer that," Larn said, nodding to himself. "At last I know what this varmint is up to."

"What?" Bill asked.

"He's fixing to make a heap of money by buying all that land for pennies and then selling to the railroad for a lot more," Larn said.

"Nonsense, son," Bill said.

But it wasn't nonsense, Fargo realized. Because now he, too, knew why Becker wanted the land so much. He remembered a poker game in Omaha, remembered a particular player who was a surveyor for the railroad. And it had been the surveyor's opinion that as soon as the territory was opened up, the railroad would push westward. Since the big locomotives needed water to run, the railroad would claim right-of-way on land near the Platte and pay a fair price to anyone who owned the land. If someone was able to obtain the land for almost no money, he'd be able to make a fortune selling to the railroad. Hundreds of thousands of dollars. Perhaps millions.

"The kid is right," Becker was saying. "Not that it matters to you one way or the other. As of right this minute, this land is mine." His hand flashed out holding a short-barreled revolver.

On cue, Schultz drew his six-shooter and trained it on Larn.

"No!" Maggy cried, putting herself in front of her husband. "I won't let you! You'll have to murder me first if you want to kill them!"

"Whatever you want, lady," Becker said, laughing. "I wasn't about to let you live anyway." He extended his arm and cocked his pistol. "Any last words? A prayer, maybe?"

"May you rot in hell!" Maggy cried.

"Hell is for paupers," Becker said.

Fargo put on his hat and stepped around the corner. "Why not try someone who can fight back?" he asked, and as he spoke, he drew with dazzling speed, his right hand like liquid lightning. Even though Becker and Schultz already had their hardware unlimbered, it was Fargo who shot first, his slug striking Becker in the chest and spinning the mastermind of the swindling operation around. Schultz got off a shot but was too overeager and missed. Fargo replied, working the trigger twice, as calm and deliberate as if he were shooting at clay targets. His slugs bored through Schultz from chin to spine and dropped the lanky killer where he stood. The remaining pair came to life, clawing in a flurry for their six-guns. Fargo, shifting, banged his Colt once and one of the gunmen staggered rearward sporting a new nostril. He flicked his Colt at the hardcase and his trigger finger was tightening when three shots sounded and the last man collapsed in a slack heap.

Fargo slowly walked over to the bodies to verify they were all dead. He blew a puff of air at the gunsmoke curling from his revolver, then began reloading.

Bill Walker was glued in place, too stupefied to speak. Maggy and Samantha were equally dumbfounded.

Jake Larn came forward, trying hard to hide his astonishment. "Three to my one!" he said softly.

"I guess we're even now," Fargo said, grinning.

"Three to my one!" Larn repeated, shaking his head. "And here I figured I was as good as you."

Samantha was the first of her family to find her voice. "Is it over, Skye?" she asked anxiously. "Is it finally, truly over?"

"Yes," Fargo answered. He twirled the Colt into his holster. "It's time to get on with our lives."

LOOKING FORWARD!
The following is the opening
section from the next novel in the exciting
Trailsman series from Signet:

THE TRAILSMAN #147
DEATH TRAILS

1860, where the Indian Territory
of Oklahoma spilled over into Texas
and where deceit spilled over into death . . . .

Fargo had expected trouble during the entire drive. If you had any trail sense you always expected trouble, especially going through the heart of the Oklahoma Indian Territory. Then, this drive had other danger signs. There weren't enough cowhands for the size of the herd, and half of them were very young and inexperienced. Yet when the trouble came, he didn't expect it. They had perhaps another two days to reach Fort Worth, he estimated, when it happened.

It came in the form of Brad Ales, the foreman of the crew and the man who had hired him. Fargo snapped awake when he heard the footsteps just before dawn and found himself staring into the barrel of a six-shot, single-action Remington-Beals revolver. A face looked down the seven-and-a-half-inch barrel at him, the face of Brad Ales, the half-moon scar on his chin strangely prominent in the last of the moonlight. Two of his men, Johnson and Olmey, stood behind him, also with their guns drawn. "Don't move," Brad Ales whispered.

Fargo ignored the command and rose onto one elbow. "What the hell is this?" he asked with a frown. Ales answered by scooping up the jeans on the ground beside the bedroll and pulling the roll of bills from one pocket.

"It's called getting robbed," the man said. "I'm taking back the money I paid you." Fargo's eyes went to the other two men. They hadn't moved. He flicked a quick glance at his own Colt where it lay in its holster and he measured the distance. Short but not short enough, he cursed silently.

"Get up," Brad Ales ordered.

"You gone crazy?" Fargo frowned.

"I've had enough of the chicken feed Rob Abbot pays. This'll make up for a half-year's work," Ales said, and at a nod of his head the other two stepped forward and grabbed Fargo by the arms. Fargo half turned, and started to twist away when the butt of the Remington crashed down on top of his head. He felt himself go down onto his knees as the world was suddenly a foggy, spinning place. He was shaking his head, trying to clear it, when the second blow of the gun slammed into him and he collapsed facedown on the ground.

The world vanished and he knew only a void, a place without sound, sight, or touch. It had all taken but seconds and he had no idea how long he'd lain unconscious, but when he woke the new dawn streaked the sky. He sat up slowly, his head throbbing and he felt the lump atop his skull and the streak of sticky, half-dried blood that ran down the side of his face. He sat for a moment, let his thoughts assemble themselves, and heard the sounds of cowhands waking. He pushed to his feet, winced, swayed for a moment, and saw the three young faces staring at him from across the ashes of the supper fire.

"Jesus, Fargo, what happened to you," Al Foster said, his unlined face wreathed in a frown.

"I was bushwhacked, right here," Fargo muttered. "By your boss."

"Brad Ales?" one of the other young hands, Ed Deeze, gasped.

"Him, Johnson, and Olmey," Fargo bit out. "You don't see them around, do you?"

"No, sir," Ed Deeze said as he let his gaze move across the herd.

"They robbed me and hightailed it," Fargo said.

"Jesus, I never figured him for that kind, but then we've only known him since the drive started," the younger man said.

"That goes for all of us," Fargo said as he pulled on his clothes. His lake blue eyes were the color of February ice. "I'm going after him . . . all of them," he said.

"Look, I'm sorry for what happened, we all are, but you ride off on us and we're in trouble. We can't bring this herd in without you," Ed Deeze said. Fargo took in their young faces, now filled with apprehension. They were right. Even one rider would make the difference, though he hadn't been hired to ride herd. "Besides, I'd think you'd want to see Rob Abbot about this," Deeze added. "I mean, Brad Ales was his man."

Fargo frowned into space for a moment. The young hand's words made sense. It also gave him a reason to stay other than feeling sorry for the trio. "All right," he said. "Let's get moving. I'll ride lead. You three cover the sides and the rear." He saw the relief flood their faces as they hurried away and he saddled the Ovaro, his head still hurting, and rode the magnificent pinto to the head of the steers. He looked back, waved, and Deeze and the other young hands began to move the steers forward. They traveled only an hour when he found a shallow stream that let the cattle drink as he cleaned the caked blood from his face. Later, moving the herd southward again, he thought of how Brad Ales had hired him.

The man had sought him out at the hotel in Wichita where he'd had a needed three-day rest after trailbreaking a large herd from far north in Nebraska Territory for Matt Dreiser. "Dreiser told me you were staying here," Brad Ales had said. "I need a trailsman for a small herd I'm taking to Fort Worth, five hundred steers but all fancy stock. I'm paying five hundred dollars."

Fargo had let a low whistle escape his lips. "That's a lot of money for that short a drive," he remarked.

"Yes, but it's all through Indian territory and I don't want to make that trip on my own," Brad Ales said. "I've all the rest of my hands. You're the last one and I'm told you're the best. Pay up front."

Five hundred dollars. Fargo murmured silently. It was an offer too good to turn down and he'd had a good rest. He'd accepted, pocketed the money, and they had started the drive south the next morning. He noticed, during the drive, that Brad Ales, Johnson, and Olmey stayed pretty much to themselves. They gave their three young, inexperienced hands little instruction in handling a herd and there was none of the kind of working camaraderie that developed on most drives. But that wasn't his concern and he spent most of the days riding far ahead of the herd as he broke trail.

Now it was clear that he should have paid more attention, but at the time he'd simply decided Brad Ales wasn't much of a trail foreman. His brow continued to furrow as he rode. There had been something strange about the bushwhacking. Ales could have killed him. It would have eliminated pursuit and he had the chance to do so? Why hadn't he? Most bushwhackers would have and Brad Ales had the cruelty in his face for it. Yet he hadn't. The anomaly stayed with Fargo as he rode until he finally put it aside and concentrated on the terrain in front of him. It was mostly flat, but a line of low sandstone dunes rose up at his right. They were drawing close enough to Fort Worth and he had all but dismissed any further chance of Indian trouble. They'd been lucky in that regard. Suddenly he reined to a halt and his lips drew back in a grimace.

The line of unshod pony prints crossed his path, led to the sandstone dunes, and Fargo swung from the Ovaro and knelt on the ground. He pressed his fingers into the tracks and swore silently. Nothing dry and crumbling about them. They were firm and fresh, not more than a few hours old, he guessed as he returned to the saddle. Dismissing Indian trouble had been premature, a case of wishful thinking. He turned the horse around and slowly rode back to the herd.

Ed Deeze and the other two young men came forward to

meet him, their eyes questioning. "Trouble, maybe, Indian pony prints ahead," Fargo said.

"How many?" Deeze questioned.

"Can't say for sure. They were riding single-file and left overlapping prints," Fargo said. "Six to eight, I'd guess."

"You think they'll come after the herd?" Deeze asked.

"Only to stampede them and pick us off," Fargo said.

Deeze winced. "If they stampede we'll never round them up."

"That depends," Fargo said and Deeze frowned. "Nobody can completely control a stampede, but we can do some things."

"Like what?" Deeze questioned.

"They'll try to stampede the herd off in all directions. That's what we don't want," Fargo said.

"How do we stop that?"

"We stampede them," Fargo said and saw the younger man's brows lift. "That'll give us some control. We set them off running together and they'll pretty much stay together. That's the way with cattle. We stay with them until they run themselves out."

"If we can stay alive," Deeze mumbled.

"Right," Fargo said. "Spread out and move them." He took a position just behind the center of the herd while the three younger men moved outward. It was a small herd and Fargo was grateful for that. They'd be more inclined to stay together having traveled as a cohesive unit. The big, sprawling herds never did develop any unity. Fargo's eyes swept the sandstone formations as they drove the cattle forward. If the Indians were behind the sandstone they could be Wichita, Osage, or even Kiowa. The Kiowa had a habit of ranging far and wide. But they could also be Comanche. He hoped not.

They were reaching the end of the sandstone formations when the barely clad horsemen swept into sight, a thousand or so yards ahead of them. Eight, he counted, as they crossed in front of the approaching herd and he glimpsed one brave wearing a full beaded choker with a tie decorated with Osage markings. Fargo was grateful for that. An Osage arrow could kill you as dead as a Comanche arrow, but he'd do battle with the Osage over the Comanche anytime. He glanced to his side and saw Ed Deeze and the others watching him. "Stay low in the saddle and stay with the herd. Don't drop back. Run inside them if you have to," Fargo said as he drew his Colt. "Now let's send them."

He raised the revolver and sent a scattershot pattern of bullets into the air and heard Deeze and the other two men do the same. The sudden sharp explosion of sound at their very backs was all the cattle needed. With a roar of bellowing sound they stampeded, straight ahead, a mass of thundering hoofs and horns. Fargo spurred the Ovaro with them, riding at the very heels of the racing steers as he flattened himself in the saddle. He saw the Osage wheel their ponies and race off to both sides of the stampeding herd. A quick glance showed Ed Deeze and the other two young hands keeping up with the steers, also low in their saddles. Fargo fought the bounce of the galloping horse under him as he reloaded, and when he raised the Colt again he steadied his hand, waited, let one of the Osage come into his sights, and fired.

The Osage flew from his pony and Fargo swung the Colt, found another target, and fired. The attacker tried to turn away, but he was too late and the heavy bullet tore his side open. Fargo saw him disappear from view and he ducked lower as two rifle shots tore over his head. A few of the Osage had rifles, but most were firing arrows as they gathered themselves to race alongside the stampeding herd. Fargo saw another go down, but not from his gun, and he pressed the Ovaro forward through a space that opened up between two steers. He could see the three young hands still bobbing up and down amid the racing steers, and he glimpsed an Osage drop back to swing in behind him. He half turned in the saddle, the Colt raised as he clung to the reins with one hand. The Indian came into sight swinging his pony around to bring up at the rear of the herd. Fargo fired, but just as the Ovaro swerved to avoid colliding with one of the steers, and he saw the brave clutch at his shoulder but stay on his pony as he turned away.

Fargo returned his attention to staying with the still-racing steers, then brought the Ovaro back a pace as the cattle closed ranks in front of him. He glimpsed Ed Deeze off to his right but didn't have time to look for the others as he had to again pull away from the swerving cattle. They were slowing, he saw, and for the most part, still together. They continued to slow, losing wind and power, panic fading with tired muscles. Fargo saw Ed Deeze, then the other two hands, rise in their saddles. His gaze swept past them to where the Osage was riding away, unwilling to lose more warriors in what had been, from the start, something less than a deadly attack. Once again, Fargo was glad they had not been the Comanche.

"Cover the flanks," he called out to Deeze. "Keep them together so they don't wander off." He let the Ovaro fall back and then raced the horse around the edge of the slowing herd until he was ahead of them. He rode back and forth in front of the lead steers and saw them slow further and finally come to a halt, breathing heavily. He heard Ed Deeze's shouts as he herded straying steers back to the main herd, and finally there was only the heavy breathing of the cattle as they stood still. "We were lucky," Fargo said to Ed Deeze as the younger man rode up to him.

"Stampeding the herd at them took them by surprise. They never got untracked," Deeze said.

Fargo's eyes moved across the herd. "Let them rest for an hour and then move them slowly. I'll ride on," he said and moved the Ovaro away at a walk. The Oklahoma terrain stayed mostly flat as he rode on, his eyes scanning the ground. But he found no new pony prints, and after one more night, they were driving the herd into Fort Worth. He asked questions, found the Rob Abbot spread at the south end of town, three big corrals and a cluster of warehouses, stables, and a large, slate-shingled main house. Corral hands opened the gates as the three young hands drove the herd inside. "Where do I find Rob Abbot?" Fargo asked one of the men.

"In the main house," the man said. "I'm sure he's watched you ride in."

Fargo nodded and rode to the slate-roofed house where a man stepped outside as he rode to a halt and dismounted. Fargo took in a tall man, perhaps fifty, he guessed, with hair still dark, an angled face with dark and piercing eyes, a prominent nose that, with the piercing eyes, gave him a somewhat hawklike expression. "Rob Abbot?" Fargo asked.

"That's right," the man said. "Who are you?"

"Skye Fargo."

Rob Abbot frowned. "Fargo . . . the one they call the Trailsman? I've heard of you," he said.

"I'd think so, seeing as how you hired me," Fargo said.

Robert Abbot frowned back. "What are you talking about? I never hired you."

"You told Brad Ales to hire me," Fargo said.

"I never told him to hire you or anyone else but some cowhands," the man said, and Fargo felt the stab of apprehension inside himself. "By the way, where is Brad? I didn't see him ride in with you."

"He's gone. He bushwhacked me, stole back the money he'd paid me and lit out, along with Johnson and Olmey," Fargo said.

Rob Abbot stared at him. "By God, I do believe you're telling me the truth," the man said.

"Damn right I'm telling you the truth," Fargo snapped.

"Maybe you'd better come inside," Abbot said, and Fargo followed him into the living room of the house and saw a large room with a leather sofa and leather chairs, stone walls hung with Indian blankets and old muskets, a comfortable room. Abbot turned to face him with a quizzical glance, his piercing eyes probing. "You've come looking for me. You were thinking it was my responsibility because I had him hire you," he said.

"Something like that," Fargo said.

"Only it's not. I never hired you, never told him to. If I hire anyone they have a piece of paper with my name on it," the man said.

"He worked for you," Fargo tried.

"That doesn't make me responsible for every damn thing he does," Abbot countered, and Fargo's lips tightened as he had to agree with the man's reply. "But I can put together why he bushwhacked you," Abbot said.

"I'd like to hear that," Fargo said.

"He's been unhappy here lately. He asked me for a bonus if he got the herd here early, by next week. I agreed and he asked me for the money up front, said it'd make him feel better, said he wanted the feel of it in his pocket."

"You agreed again."

"Yes. He'd worked for me for a year. If it'd help make him get the herd here early I was willing to go along with it," Abbot said. "It's plain now that he used the money to hire you and then stole it back from you."

"That's what the son of a bitch did," Fargo said. "But two questions bother me. Why'd he wait till I was only two days from here and could bring the herd in?"

Abbot smiled. "That's easy. He knew if I had the herd I'd have no cause to go chasing after him."

"Then why didn't he kill me. Most bushwhackers would have?" Fargo questioned.

"That's easy, too. If he were to be caught, robbin' brings a lot less jail than murder," Abbot said.

Fargo let out a deep sigh. Abbot was right on everything. "Which all means you've got your cattle and I've got empty pockets," he said.

"I'm sorry for that, but I'm still not responsible for what happened. But I'd like to help you out. Fact is, maybe we can do each other a turn," Abbot said, his lips pursing in thought. "I've a job for a man with your skills and I'll pay real good money, more than enough to pay for the time you've lost and for what Brad Ales stole back from you."

"I'm listening," Fargo said.

"I want you to find my daughter and bring her back here to me," the man said.

Fargo thought for a moment. "I'm not much for tracking down runaways," he said.

"But you have tracked down people."

"I have."

"And it's more than that," Abbot said.

"How old is she?" Fargo asked.

"Twenty-two," Abbot said.

"Then she's old enough to do what she wants. I'd need a reason to haul her back," Fargo said.

"She stole two thousand dollars from me when she left. That'll do for a reason."

"It will for a sheriff but not for me. What's the real story?" Fargo queried. "Why do you want her back?"

Rob Abbot motioned him to come to the large window at one side of the room. "Look out there. That's Abbot Enterprises. We buy and sell cattle. Horses, too, and hogs. We run a freight line. We own storage depots. We operate two riverboats that sail the Trinity to Galveston and back and they're always loaded. It's a fine enterprise that makes good money, but it's going down the drain because of Dulcy."

"How's that?" Fargo inquired.

"Because I need her signature on every important document, on bank withdrawals, checks, credit transactions, everything. You see, the business was really my wife's, Dulcy's mother, a family business. When Clara died she wanted Dulcy to be a part of the business so she made Dulcy a partner in her will. But Dulcy never gave a damn about the business. She told me to sell out or she'd bring the whole thing down. I thought she was just talking until I found out differently."

"But she's bringing it down on her head, too. Seems like she's cutting her nose off to spite her face," Fargo said.

"She was left a small income of her own, enough to get by," Abbot said. "She's also chasing a man, a gambler who ditched her. But she still wants him. This is a terrible thing for a father to say, but Dulcy is a spoiled, unprincipled, vicious young woman who's capable of anything. I've often wondered if she wasn't more than a little twisted inside."

"You sure make her sound that way," Fargo said.

"Now you know why I have to have her brought back here and as damn soon as possible," Abbot said.

"I could bring her back and she might still refuse to sign," Fargo mentioned.

"I think once she's back here she'll sign. She always has. If not, I'll make her an offer to buy her out. I'm sure she'll go for that. But I need her here, first, and time to convince her to do what's right," the man said. "I'll pay you a thousand, half up front, the rest when you bring her in."

Fargo felt his brows lift. "That'll pay for a lot of tracking," he said. "But I still aim to get Brad Ales. He set me up, bushwhacked me, and robbed me. I don't take to any of those things much less all three together."

"I want you to forget about Brad Ales. You concentrate on finding Dulcy," Rob Abbot said.

"You send anyone else after her?" Fargo questioned.

"No. I thought she might come back on her own. I guessed wrong," Abbot said.

"How long has she been gone?"

"Three months. I had enough cash on hand to last that long," the man said.

"What's she look like?" Fargo asked.

"Tall, brown hair, brown eyes, good-looking enough," Abbot said.

"That'd fit a lot of girls," Fargo sniffed.

"I know," Abbot shrugged helplessly. "I've one lead. She had a woman friend who lived in Kempton. She might've gone there."

"That's a start," Fargo said.

"She has one favorite expression. When she gets real mad at somebody she says they're lower than snake shit," Abbot said.

"Everything helps. This gambler she's chasing. What's his name?" Fargo asked.

"I'm not sure. She never did tell me. It was always a sore point with us," the man said.

"All right, you've got a deal, mister," Fargo said. "And a herd of cattle."

"I thank you for the second one and I'm sure I'll be thanking you for the first," Abbot said. "Now I'll get your money." He hurried into another room and Fargo glimpsed what seemed to be a small office with a desk and file cabinet. He returned in moments with the roll of crisp bills that Fargo stuffed into an inside pocket in his vest. "Good luck. Time's important," Abbot said as he walked to the door with Fargo. "One last thing, and I hate to even bring this up, but I know how vicious Dulcy can be. If anything should happen to her, I mean anything real bad, I want you to bring her body back here anyway. Her mother would want her buried here on our land."

"Understood," Fargo said and strode to his horse. He rode from the Abbot layout digesting everything that had been told him. It had been quite a story. Rob Abbot plainly had little love left for his daughter, but a lot of need for her. From his words, Dulcy Abbot was a handful of hellcat. Kempton lay southwest, but Fargo sent the pinto north. Despite Abbot's instructions, he still wanted to cross paths with Brad Ales again and he took the time to return to where the herd had halted that night. It was the next morning when he finally reached the spot, just north of the small stream. He had no trouble finding the hoofprints of the three horses that had raced away to the northeast and he followed at a slow, steady trot, more hope than expectation inside him.

But hope brought its own rewards as, some half-dozen miles on, he saw the footprints turn south and stay southward. Fargo allowed himself a small smile of satisfaction. With a little luck he could settle a score of his own while pursuing a hellcat named Dulcy. He smiled again at the incongruity of the name and the young woman Rob Abbot had described. But he had learned long ago that this was a world of incongruities. He just hadn't tracked one before now.